THE FRACTURED UNIVERSE

The Fractured Universe
Copyright 2021 by David Glen Robinson, Ph.D.

This is a work of fiction. All names, characters and incidents are the product of the author's imagination or are used fictitiously. Any resemblance to current or local events or to living persons is entirely coincidental.

ISBN: 978-1-7376824-0-0

Cover Design Brian Wootan
Editor Mindy Reed, The Authors' Assistant
Interior Design Danielle H Acee, The Authors' Assistant

Printed in the United States of America

THE FRACTURED UNIVERSE

a novel

David Glen Robinson, Ph.D.

1

Roller stood in a brushy meadow—what ranchers call a pasture—peering closely at black-on-black instrumentation. This was no pastoral scene. The man shook with anxiety as he ran his eyes all over the control boards, trying to mesh video and audio between different instruments set out on the pasture grasses. He'd make sure the next generation of his mega-tablet would run AV on a single circuit. Forget all these black boxes.

Angry and fearful, he wondered why he, a wildlife biologist, was doing what an audio engineer should be doing. "Because an audio engineer wouldn't set foot out here to record will-o'-the-wisps," he answered himself. He'd rather be studying freshwater leeches in mountain streams. He tried to calm himself. PhDs weren't allowed to look and act this confused. Anyway, his reform school dropout employee, Laney Joe Ferguson, could have set this whole system up in a few minutes, and he couldn't even read a circuit diagram. Talent is where you find it.

It was just then getting dark enough. Roller checked the cables running out to the power pack. He could see Alan Silvy in the distance removing the last of the marker stakes for the magnetometry and ground-penetrating radar transects. The equipment and crews had already left. Earlier, the supervisor had shaken his head at him as the crews departed, so Roller knew the results were negative. He raged, seeing once again that the scientific method was a swamp of disappointment and fear—a true slough of despond. Roller sighted the cameras on Alan before the man walked out of frame. Roller tried to keep a grip on himself.

Roller thought he had succeeded in the final adjustments and was ready, but his anxiety cascaded torrentially. He thought of his main funding source, the Berkish Foundation, and their demands for results. The voice of Don Berkish rang in his memory. "Science in the academy and science out here in the real world are two different things. Out here, we want results for commercial gain, not equivocal-positive or suggestive-negative. You just have to explain the Marfa Lights in a way that furthers the reputation of Berkish Foundation as a pioneering research and technology corporation. We're chasing Musla Corp., you know." Roller had decided then and there not to tell Berkish about the miniaturized Tesla coil in his mega-tablet that served as its power source. He wanted to prove that science could make the world a better place—no more atomic bombs. Sadly, it had been taken over by commercial greed. *Money kills idealism,* he thought.

Roller's Berkish funding had been spent with the completion of the magnetometry and ground-penetrating radar effort. The engineering company he had contracted with for the work had typically high rates. Roller looked into the viewfinders, holes no blacker than his heart, certainly. A red ball expanded like an inflating balloon to fill the viewfinder. He jumped back startled and shaking again. He could see more lights out in the field that weren't from his cameras.

The red orb drifted slowly out of frame leftward. Two gray orbs, dimmer and smaller than the red sphere, followed it. Five golden pin lights, incandescent like small Christmas lights, appeared farther back in the pasture. Roller grabbed his mega-tablet and began recording additional video with it. The red orb seemed to drift back and forth about five feet above the pasture. Then it vibrated rapidly and burst in a corona of sparks.

Roller looked for smoke or small fires starting in the pasture grass, but there were none. "Alan, are you getting any of this?" he shouted to Alan Silvy, who stood about fifty feet away. Silvy merely pointed with one hand to the digital video recorder braced against his shoulder by the other hand.

The dimmer gray orbs moved apart in opposite directions but also about five feet off the ground. One of them dimmed out slowly, followed seconds later by the other light. By this time, the pin lights had disappeared as well. The pasture fell to darkness. The only light was the waning moon with thin, silent clouds scudding across it. The tension grew so thick it could have been carved with an ice cream scoop. Then a dull yellowish-gray light appeared, moving in slow, diagonal zigzags across the field as though blown around by light breezes. But there were no ground-level breezes. The zigzag light disappeared without fading first and was replaced by a gray light which pulsed on and off as though trying and failing to light. The light went out after a few seconds. Soon two dim gray lights appeared, along with a dull red globe. The lights moved slowly and at random with respect to each other though there were no ground-level winds to push them around. They all dimmed to darkness, and fifteen minutes later, without any more sightings, it was clear that the performance for the evening was at an end. But Roller and Alan had more work to do.

Roller still had the shakes when they tore down the recording equipment for the night. Roller felt weak and ill. He was both satisfied that he had made a scientific recording of the lights and frightened by their otherworldliness. Too bad about the magnetometry and ground-penetrating radar. He couldn't shake his fear. He firmly believed that the lights were a real-world, materialistic phenomenon, explainable with cause and effect principles. But that was top-brain stuff. In his gut, he felt that the lights were sentient somehow and coming at him with intent. He was still shivering, and he hurried to the SUV to get his overcoat and stand near its solidity and another human being, even if it was Alan Silvy.

"Keep your distance, dude," Silvy said.

Snide bastard. Roller admired people with the confidence to lead with their defensiveness. Identifying contradictions in people always cheered him up.

"I need food and rest," he said.

"That makes two of us," Alan replied. "Been out here too long."

The mega-tablet rang, and the ID read "Sigmadon Berkish."

"Hello, Don," Roller said. "We had a good light show tonight. The Marfa Lights were out in full force. The magnetometry and ground-penetrating radar are done—" The silence on the other end of the line made Roller pause.

"Roller, why didn't you tell us you were no longer working for Alford Global when you received our grant?" Berkish's tone was conversational.

"They released us after we sent you the application. We also stated carefully that Alford in no way would support or sponsor our work. We're independent," Roller said.

"Independent, schmindependent. Don't you know we require institutional support to buffer us when things go wrong with you crazy scientists? And who's 'we?'"

"Mahan Faringway. His name's on the application."

"I see," Berkish said. "We're pulling your grant. Send back all the money and any equipment we loaned you. And in the future, don't let Mahan Faringway anywhere near any little projects you may start."

Roller couldn't think. "*Tck...tck,*" he stammered. "I demand arbitration! And what about Berkish standing at the leading edge of knowledge?"

"That's not on me," Berkish said. "The public relations department writes all the lies."

"But we've already spent the..."

Click. Berkish had broken the connection.

Roller's shakes got worse as a brisk wind picked up. He was verging on hypothermia. He glanced into the pasture to see if any lights appeared to sail around on the gusts. They didn't.

They threw everything into the SUV and drove off, with Alan Silvy at the wheel. Roller felt weak and disoriented, and he just wanted out of the wind, which was rising now to the near-nightly storm level.

"Have you called Faringway, yet?" Silvy asked. He had a permanent squint in one eye.

"No, I haven't," Roller said. "We both know he'll just start screaming. Still, if the project's done, he has to know."

Roller moved the mega-tablet onto his lap to make the call.

The primary idea of Roller's scientific research experiment had been to shoot video of the Marfa Lights and the Aurora Borealis at the same time, after placing cameras very close to the same line of longitude. If the two phenomena were related, then aspects of their observable behavior, viewed simultaneously, might match—intensity, color patterns, sudden appearance, or extinction—even though their general appearance was dissimilar. The Marfa Lights were where they were, so the Aurora Borealis viewing point had to be chosen far to the north, as close to the same longitude as Marfa. Roller had chosen a point east of Regina, Saskatchewan, in a farmer's wheat field and hired two college students to video their northern lights at the same times as Roller shot the Marfa Lights in Texas.

The Aurora Borealis revealed part of Earth's electromagnetic field when its energy became visible light at the earth's poles. Roller hypothesized that perhaps a spike of energy became diverted through metallic ore veins below the Earth's surface and popped out visibly in Marfa, and *voilá*, the Marfa Lights. Roller couldn't think of a voltmeter large enough to stick into the earth to measure the energy flows. Other ideas might emerge when more data came in.

The geology of the region very likely had much to do with the Marfa Lights. The silver, copper, and gold deposits at Shafter had not yet been explored fully, but the mercury deposits south near Big Bend National Park had played out centuries before. The empty mines left only the shaky little ghost town of Terlingua. This was why he had spent the Berkish money on magnetometry and ground-penetrating radar, to see if there was anything subsurface that might partly explain the lights, but mostly to eliminate unfruitful avenues. Now he just thought of it as a waste.

The mountains east of the brownish Marfa plain held a sort of indigo glow. The oddly shaped peaks seemed to enjoy the light show below. The moon above gave the peaks a metallic luster shaded briefly by the silver shreds of clouds masking it. It reminded Roller of the lace fabric often used for masquerade ball masks. This was such a mysterious land, and Marfa was a mysterious small town in the middle of nowhere with a tiny art village in the center of it.

At the moment, the scenery was competing with Faringway screaming through the mega-tablet for Roller's attention.

"We'll find some money somewhere, Faringway," he shouted into the mega-tablet. Mercifully, just then, Faringway broke the connection. *Why did Berkish say that about Faringway?*

"What makes you think that video will reveal what this spooky stuff is all about?" Alan asked, a trifle more truculent than normal.

"Video's only a small part of it," Roller replied, happy to start getting Alan off his paranormal speculations about the lights.

"Well, why can't you point a fancy spectroscope at them like they point at different planets and just say what kind of fart gas they are pooting all over the pasture?" Silvy had suddenly become very talkative.

"The lights don't seem to be chemical, Alan. They're more like some form of electromagnetic energy—just plain light." He'd explained the difference between chemical energy and electromagnetics several times, and Alan never seemed to get it. *Hmmm.* It struck Roller that maybe Roller was actually the one who didn't get it. But then maybe he had too much self-doubt.

Alan gave a cross between a sigh and a snort. Then he threw his hands in the air in a defeated gesture. "Care to explain so I can understand?"

"Keep, keep your hands on the wheel, Alan," Roller said. He had started to accept that explaining the lights was going to be the principal challenge with Alan, but talking about the mystery clarified Roller's thinking about it. That was why he tolerated Alan. He wondered if Alan tolerated him in turn. The same went for Mahan Faringway, who was a willing partner in their outrageous adventure in rebel science but who held everyone in his life at arm's length. He knew Faringway was going to leave him holding the bag on the grant money.

Alan Silvy drifted with the desert winds—as blown and empty as a zephyr. He lived in the desert on nothing but casino winnings when he had them. He'd learned a lot about desert foraging for those times when he didn't. It didn't make sense to call Alan homeless in these wide-open spaces where there weren't many homes. Homelessness was an urban construct.

Alan told Roller he had made a sacrifice for love years ago and had no more trades to make in life. It was all take it or leave it for him now—no reason to pay rent, no reason to bathe. Roller considered Silvy the freest, most liberated individual he had ever met, but he had won his liberation through crushing loss.

Alan's zen-like quest to quench all desire was stopped or slowed down by one persistent personality trait, and that trait was curiosity. He had a lot of it. He told Roller and everyone else that his curiosity led to food or winning hands of blackjack in Vegas. By now, he had an immense memory archive of desert plants and small fauna and how their lives cycled through the seasons. He also had a few wins in the casinos, none large enough to come to the attention of management. Roller could easily see that Alan Silvy was the optimal dog, not too large, not too small, and just clever enough to survive.

They talked until Alan drove into the informal campground a rancher was allowing them to use—a corner of a field behind a gate where they could park and pitch their camp tent. It was the research campaign headquarters.

Alan trundled off to the tent, unzipped the doorway, and entered. Roller heard him fall without ceremony onto his sleeping bag. He wanted to know if Faringway and the couple, Laney Joe and Terri Serekova, were having any luck recording ghost voices down in Terlingua, but he knew better than to call again. Roller thought privately that ghost hunting research was stupid, but he knew that the brilliant, if acerbic, Faringway was an asset to any team, so he was willing to put up with a lot. Roller reflected that it was his own overwhelming curiosity that tied him both to Silvy and to Faringway. He wanted to see what they could create. He knew it was a lot, but dammit, there were limits. He wondered if he was nearing those limits and what would happen—to them and to him—when he hit the bumpers.

2

Terri Serekova grew skeptical of any electronic voice phenomena, or EVPs, the farther she walked through the narrow mine gallery. The former mercury mine was well lit so as not to frighten the tourists. Terri walked comfortably through the rocky tunnel, her narrow hips and slender legs striding along without brushing the dusty rocks on either side. Laney Joe Ferguson behind her was not so fortunate. "Wait up. Oof...ow," he said. He was not much wider than Terri, but he wasn't nearly as coordinated. The sharp rock edges caught at him and the equipment bags.

The gallery was incredibly dusty, and the fine-grained yellowish sandstone took sharp angles when it had been chopped through by the mercury miners. The rock also released dust when rubbed. Terri pulled her bandana up over her nose. The mine operators pumped a little air through the galleries so they could operate a tourist attraction, but stale seemed to win the battle over fresh.

The cinnabar-red deposits of mercury ore she was looking for were nowhere to be seen. Terri twisted her lips as she examined the EVP recorder; this didn't seem like a very rich mine. The sandstone on either side of the walkway was uniformly jagged. Any color variation was coated with dust. She walked on with Laney Joe doggedly behind her.

The mine tour guide waddled up to them. He was large. She could tell he had learned from years of practice to walk sideways through the mine. "A substantial vein was encountered in this direction," he said. Three walkways led in different directions from the indicated alcove.

"The miners followed the vein wherever it led them," the guide continued. "The tunnel there," he gestured, "led to the end of this mine—very deep. Ten more dollars to get to the bottom. Definitely a lot of ghosts." He smiled.

Terri gave him a sharp look, catching his inflection of mockery. Laney Joe watched her body language and waited for her to look at him. When she did, he returned a quick, sharp head shake from behind the tour guide. "We're done," she said to the tour guide, not wanting to discuss with a cynic whether ghosts actually exist. She turned to Laney Joe. "I'm not getting a peep from the earbuds."

Laney Joe sighed, relieved, and took one last reference flash photo before turning back. Terri and Laney Joe were finding out that research had many dead ends. Laney Joe, in particular, applied his reform school skills of reading the intent of the other inmates from their body language. Terri was aware of those highly intuitive skills and thought they applied in important ways to this field of crazy science. She remembered, from his stories, that he generally counseled the teenage boys in reform school to take better courses of action. He got a lot of practice at that and showed wisdom beyond his years. Of course, the authorities never recognized him for what he did, even by the time he was released. They couldn't understand why the violence level went up after Laney Joe Ferguson left. Mahan Faringway was similarly oblivious to Laney Joe's skills, but Roller was highly appreciative.

The drive back to Terlingua, where Faringway was currently camped in a small hotel, was ten or twelve miles. Laney Joe took a few photographs from the passenger side while Terri drove Faringway's SUV. "Maybe the tourist mine failed," he said, "because it was too far from the center of the richest ore deposits."

"Right," said Terri, "and maybe the mine was later opened for tours because it hadn't had any cave-ins. Perhaps mercury deposits interfered with the structural integrity of the sandstone surrounding them, so rich mines caved in a lot."

"Yes," he said, "and then there's greed. They dug out the rich galleries so the interior space was more open, and the ceiling beams couldn't hold up the ceilings. It was before mine safety laws, and there was a war on."

"And because they fell in, they were never safe enough to open later for tourists like us to record the ghost calls of lost miners. We could only investigate where there weren't any lost miners." They laughed at the irony. "This was another fool's errand assigned by Faringway suffering from his brainyosis," Terri said. A feeling of unease that had hit her in the mine came back to Terri. Without any spirits to attack her, she figured it must have been the remnant mercury dust and powder, as little of it as there was. It was a sudden feeling of not belonging here, dislocation, but with a warm feeling of adventure. She'd had it before in erotic dreams. Mercury was the poison of all the mad hatters. Could it poison her dreams? As she had many times before, she gave a silent prayer of thanks that Laney Joe was in her life as a ward against life's evil. And she had seen a lot of that in her young life.

Laney Joe Ferguson glanced over at her. He couldn't remember a time before Terri, though that wasn't so long ago. He thought of her as his savior. His parents were effectively invisible, so negligent and absent in raising him they'd gradually disappeared from any mental image he might have had of them. The tough parts of his life began early, in middle school. He was definitely in the school-to-prison pipeline. He'd landed in juvie twice and logged a net of about six months in county awaiting trial. His parents laughed it off, joking that he must like jail food better than their food at home. All he learned from his stints on paper was that he had to get out, to leave. Don't steal, don't fight, just leave. Forget high school. He saved enough in wage labor to buy a bus ticket to gain his liberation after paying off his warrant with the help of a public defender. He remembered how his heart sang when they pulled out of the sterile bus station on that bus to anywhere. How he could be so scarred with such a gentle personality was a mystery to all who knew him, most recently Terri. He knew he had inner skills and hidden talents. Outside of Terri, the world couldn't see them at all. The turmoil of life had painted him thoroughly, but the tints of rage had drained away over the years. He knew discovering Terri was part of his healing. She was really all he wanted in this bizarre job. Even her flaws were attractive—the first two toes on both of her feet were not straight but curved toward each other. It came from going *en pointe* in ballet at too early an age. Terri was taken into a professional ballet company as a teenager; she became a star, and that was all she knew growing up. Naturally, a time came when she had to find a life, any life. She left. It was no coincidence that Terri and Laney Joe found each other. They'd simply found life.

The only modern hotel near Terlingua squatted down the hill from the falling-in structures of the village. It was a one-story concrete block building—dull, modern strip shopping center architecture—not much more than a line of six rooms stretching into the desert.

They arrived after dark. Terri drove up in front of Mahan Faringway's room, team headquarters in Terlingua. They got out of the SUV, stretched, and knocked on the door. Faringway gestured them into his room. "Idiot Roller got our grant pulled," he said. They both recoiled, knowing that Faringway's emotional fragility was just juvenile enough to allow him to take out his anger on the innocent.

"Let's tear everything down and load it all in the vehicle for the trip back to Marfa. But first let's play back everything—the photos, electronic voice phenomena, and monitoring. I forgot to ask if you got anything in the tourist mine."

"Nope. Nothing." Terri was curt, not wanting to get into it.

Faringway made a throwaway gesture with his arm. "That's what I get using Roller's crew of reform school dropouts."

Laney Joe wasn't having it. "Ummm, Terri graduated from a dance academy, and she's never been arrested."

Faringway gave an evil snicker, "Oh, right, a *dance* academy. The pinnacle of education. I stand corrected."

"You expect great work out of us trash when you talk like that?" Laney Joe asked. Faringway gave him a glare.

Just like the guards in juvie, Laney Joe thought. His stronger feeling, however, was the crawling creeps. Based on his feelings now, he thought Terlingua was full of ghosts, and the feeling was not one he'd had in the tourist mine. Just here. He knew Terri had some depressing feelings in the mine, but who wouldn't in such a place? This was not the same. As usual, he felt no obligation to share that with anyone around him, except Terri. He noticed her stealing glances at him, so she knew he had something flitting through his head. They'd talk later.

Terri knew Laney Joe had something he wouldn't tell. She couldn't blame him for being so withdrawn after being kicked around his entire life. Faringway just treated him like a jailbird. Terri was more interested in Laney Joe than all the theoretical ghosts in Terlingua.

She threw up her arms for peace. "Hey, guys, we have to work together just a little longer, or we'll be stuck here in Terlingua, unemployed. And who knows? Maybe Roller will have solid ideas about renewed funding by the time we get back there."

Faringway seemed to alternate between annoyance and distraction. He bit his tongue and remained silent, knowing that unleashing his tongue usually unleashed more of his anger. Terri and Laney Joe debriefed him in detail on the visit to the tourist mine over convenience store cuisine. In the mine, they had captured no electronic voice phenomena, no paranormal events, no cold spots, no apparitions. Nor did Faringway record anything elsewhere in Terlingua. They loaded up the record photos of the electronic setup in the hotel room on two computer monitors.

"We have to recalibrate the cameras. Anything that might be perceived as a ghost image would just be a flaw in one of Roller's cheap cameras," Faringway said, fuming at Laney Joe. Faringway believed in nothing at the moment—not ghosts, not murder victims, not science, not even himself.

3

Roller clicked off with the Canadians in Saskatchewan after the check-in call. They recorded the aurora as normal, nothing special to report. Alan had started to snore in the tent. As an independent researcher, Roller could claim no position in a university or advanced research lab, but when thrust into nature by the lack of that kind of employment, he grew unexcelled credentials of experience and a whole lot of freedom of thought. A degree of bitterness rode along with that, sometimes holding the reins. Conducting research as a pampered college researcher was a lot easier than this.

Roller turned away from the tent, stepped to the SUV, and slid into the driver's seat out of the wind. The door closed and blocked out Alan's snores. Almost immediately, however, thunder rolled…and rolled and rolled. Roller found that odd, seeing no lightning flashes.

Roller found it peculiar and unexplainable why he found Alan, a kindred soul, across the divides of class and culture. Roller seemed to sit at his feet like a child listening to his grandfather's stories. But Alan's stories were about the kick-around side of life, the flip side. They started in gray, dark, brick-and-concrete, inner-city alleys and crash landed in sandy, oven-hot, sun-blasted arroyos in the Southwest. Roller respected Alan's knowledge that came from that world, a world that Roller's middle-class upbringing had denied him. Although Roller's respect for Alan colored his view of the man, trust was not one of the tints.

Roller viewed the night's progression of mysteries on playback on Silvy's video recorder. The lights never seemed to have pattern. Maybe he shouldn't be looking for them. Maybe their randomness was the pattern. Roller finished a stick of beef jerky and slumped over the SUV's steering wheel.

Things were not settling down in Terlingua. The hotel room was a tempest in a bottle. A little boy tapped on the front window. "Can I come in now?" the boy named Yanni called from outside.

Faringway was snarling and out of sorts. "Don't let that brat in here," he said. He jerked the media out of the video monitor and examined it for malfunctions while Terri pulled up the metadata on the photos on the comp. She frowned at Faringway and waved at the little boy from behind her back. Laney Joe quietly walked to the door and let in the boy with a finger to his lips for quiet.

Yanni had wandered up to them while they were touring around Terlingua. He didn't say where he lived nor did he name his parents. When they pressed him, he gave his name as Yelbert Yannington. Yanni seemed natural as a nickname. He was a bright-eyed seven-year-old who liked to hang out with them, play, and not ask too many questions. Faringway asked him to go home several times. Yanni just looked pained and stayed out of the way. Laney Joe and Terri saw themselves in Yanni—a fellow seeker of life who hadn't been given much of a pathway into it. Now they were making their own paths, helping and seeking help from other travelers along the way. Terri and Laney Joe had Yanni's back from the first.

Yanni had told them earlier that he didn't have a home. He simply rode around in a minivan from place to place with his parents. No schooling—he could read packaged food labels, but not the ingredient lists on the back. He didn't know how his parents got money to fill the gas tank, and they did not tell him. Yanni was tired of running with them.

Terri, seeing him now quiet and hungry in the corner, determined that he would eat with them whenever they had food. She found an energy bar and gave it to him, then turned back to Faringway's chaotic mess. Yanni slipped back outside.

All of a sudden, everything seemed to blur slightly, as when a person is shaken harshly and their eyes lose focus. The instrumentation on the folding table clicked randomly as red warning lights came on and power-off buzzers reported. The computers restarted. The lights stayed on. Faringway swore in frustration. When everyone recovered, they checked and restarted the machines. Maybe it was a slight earthquake, an artifact of the era of petroleum hydro-fractionation.

"We have to get out of here," Faringway ordered. No one took exception.

Just then, the giant nightly storm broke overhead. This time, the lights flashed and went out as the storm's leading-edge dust cloud blew through, followed by spitting rain that turned the dust to mud.

More confusion, more wind, and vicious lightning. Laney Joe quietly opened the door. Yanni splashed back inside, crying. Laney Joe steered him to the bathroom and draped a towel over his head, wrapped another around him for dry warmth. Yanni didn't have a change of clothing.

They dismantled Faringway's paranormal research setup. It took a while to grip all the cables and load the equipment cases, and they became soaked in the rain carrying the equipment to the SUV. Laney Joe worked like a man obsessed. He seemed to know where everything belonged, packed it all up and loaded it efficiently in what seemed like five minutes. Faringway took note of his efficiency but said nothing. Camping gear, clothing, and blankets went on top of the black boxes. Yanni, in towels, perched on the top of the mountain of gear.

The team was only too happy to pile into Faringway's SUV once it was loaded.

"Get that brat out of here," said Faringway.

"No," said Terri and Laney Joe in unison.

Faringway snarled and pressed the ignition.

The highway out of town led to the Rio Grande and joined another highway. The researchers' intent was to drive upstream in the SUV to the town of Presidio and then to turn northeast into the mountains and onto the Marfa Plain.

The frustrated ghost hunters looked back to see the Chisos mountains of the Big Bend etching indigo peaks against the night. The moon had risen above them, masked by ragged silver clouds, the remains of the storm. One last lightning burst flared furiously, and a chip of its fire arced outward in a hexagon shape—very odd—a pinkish windowpane of energy jostling the stars.

4

Roller was still awake when the SUV arrived at the Marfa camp. A rear door popped open, and a naked boy leaped out with a towel tied around his neck, his arms out, running-flying like a superhero in nothing but flip-flops and the towel. He ran to a far corner of the encampment, leaned back and relieved himself, striking a pose like some cherub filling a pool where wishes cost a penny.

Laney Joe laughed and walked up to a visibly startled Roller. "When the sun rises, we'll buy him some clothes at a store in town."

Roller set down his mega-tablet. "*Tck*. There are extra blankets in the tent, too. Superhero shorts and T-shirts should suit his tastes nicely." Roller handed over some cash for the clothing.

Faringway walked up sleepy and cold after the long drive but appeared to Roller to be upset far beyond mere physical discomfort, which of course, he was.

"How was it in Terlingua?" asked Roller.

"Unexplained," said Faringway. "Same to you in Marfa?"

"The lights have been good, but Canada doesn't have much to match," Roller said. "Of course, it will all have to wait until we can run the videos with the time stamps matched up."

"Or until you gain a method that doesn't suck," Faringway said. Roller recoiled at the sharpness of tone.

Roller was not emotionally prepared for criticism. After a flush of anger, he thought, *My ego doesn't allow it.* Outwardly, he took a deep breath that turned into a sigh. "Let's talk in my car. Nobody's sleeping in there." Laney Joe, Terri, and Yanni had nested in Faringway's SUV.

Faringway climbed into the vehicle and stretched out in the passenger seat beside Roller. He lowered the seatback in the recliner function, and Roller did the same. "When we leave Marfa, you and I must go our separate ways," Faringway started. "The crew is yours, of course, and you have to pay them without assistance from me."

Roller was beaten and didn't have much to say, but he did realize Don Berkish would approve of this plan. Roller still didn't know why.

"I'm sorry you've had it with me," Roller offered politely, "but listen, Faringway, I have high-quality video of the lights from last night, and we have baseline data from the ground-penetrating radar and magnetometry. The stuff is negative, but you have to whittle away the negative hypotheses, so what's left is reality. The point is, I believe I can use the hard data to gain more funding and pay off the technicians."

"You believe the Marfa Lights and the Aurora Borealis are the same thing?" Faringway gave Roller a visually sarcastic, fixed stare. Some of his professors and all of his students knew it well. Most called it The Look. A few called it The Glare.

Faringway snorted.

Roller ignored it and went on. "But you prefer to record what you think are ghost voices—with unproven electronic technology…for profit? Buddy, it almost sounds like a latter-day shell game."

"What did you just say about support?" Faringway's finger was in the air again. "How are you paying for your so-called research on the Marfa Lights now, Roller? Serious question."

"*Tck...tck.* Um—the last of the residuals from the book and the savings from the job with Alford Global. And I'll be looking for more grants."

"That's not enough to pay your dropout crew. And when Berkish gets through talking to the other granters, they won't even take your calls. Don't forget, you have to send back the money you've already spent. My research at least will pay for itself, but yours? How will you support yourself after the so-called conclusive results are in? I have a feeling you'll be holding an EVP recorder in a cavern, too."

"Recording the wind blowing through cobwebs," said Roller.

Faringway laughed out loud, pulled a small EVP recorder out of his pocket, and slapped it down on Roller's thigh.

"What's this?" Roller asked.

"It is your first EVP recorder. You'll be needing it soon."

Roller put the small black device in his pocket, saying nothing in hopes of ending the conversation. He settled further into a reclining position.

The following day was spent resupplying and buying clothes for Yanni in town. Faringway ran his computer off a power pack and kept his face in the monitor for most of the daylight hours. He lingered, wanting to see the lights in the evening. Roller spread maps seeking inspiration. Eventually Alan said, "Time to go to the rest stop."

They had to set up early, not knowing if the lights would show or not. The highway department knew Roller was conducting a study of the lights—not the first by any means—and they didn't care as long as Roller's viewing station kept open the public's access to the concrete-walled visitors' terrace. Roller and Alan set up below the curved concrete wall in front of and below the viewing telescopes. The view was fine. Most visitors remained ignorant of their presence.

When the sun went down, the lights came out. Roller suspected they came out in daytime, but their lower intensity couldn't compete with daylight. Faringway and the rest of the team sat in the grass, treating the event like a picnic. As predicted, Yanni sported a T-shirt with a garish superhero face—a half robot, half organic beast. Terri and Laney Joe had thoughtfully shoveled him into little boy jeans, long pants to buffer his propensity for running through cactus. Laney Joe helped Alan Silvy, now completing tasks even before being asked or told how to proceed.

The lights were abundant, but they all vibrated, pulsed, or strobed at high frequencies. Sometimes the pulsing was all together, in harmony; sometimes they broke apart into solos. The only consistency was the appearing and disappearing randomness Roller had come to expect. The effect of the display was alternating nausea and hypnosis.

The mega-tablet flashed with a call from Canada. The voice on the speaker told them that the students weren't setting up video tonight. A bizarre, unseasonal arctic air mass was clawing at Saskatchewan and heading south. That was enough for Roller. "Let's tear it down, go back to camp, and start the campfire."

Two hours later, Alan testily threw the last grocery store log on the fire. "Can you call this science when you take every weather shutdown?" he growled. Laney Joe, Terri, and Yanni worked through the last of the take-out ribs and ignored him. The nightly West Texas storm was blowing in earlier than the one the night before. As always, the dust cloud, yesterday's mud, blew ahead of the wind and the continuous rumbling thunder.

More ominous to Roller was the tone of Silvy's voice. "Research experiments never happen in straight-line textbook fashion, Alan," Roller said. "You have to roll with the punches and keep your data clean."

"Seriously? Is that why your experiments never find publication? Can you still take that approach when you are researching in debt with the books in the red?" Silvy glared, furious. He'd been learning sarcasm and facial expression from Faringway.

Roller flinched, stung. "*Tck...tck.* It's closer to the nature of science than you can accept, apparently."

Faringway snickered, entertained. He *tck-tcked* along with Roller in mockery.

"You don't have a scientific experiment; you have a science fair project." Silvy got up and left the circle of relative warmth, walking away with the step of one who has embraced the desert many times before and returns to it as home.

As Roller watched Silvy walk away, the wind stopped. The smoke rose from the campfire straight up in a narrow column. It climbed at least a thousand feet before Roller could no longer follow it.

Then silence fell across the darkened landscape like an invisible blanket. Roller and the team stopped their talking and looked around curiously. Even Yanni stopped making noises. No scratchy crickets or buzzing mosquitoes interrupted the silence. An ember in the fire broke, the crack of it heard all over the camp.

The TV screen of reality shivered briefly. They'd seen and felt it before, like an adjustment to the monitor picture. This one was accompanied by a distinct *click.* The crickets and other insects hopped and flew madly at random.

Then the ground shook in a brief earthquake. A rumble came out of the mountains, rising in volume. The wind picked up, its whistling shattering the silence. It blew from everywhere.

This is not natural, not right, Laney Joe thought. He picked up a blanket and took it to sit on in a low spot in the brush. The vehicles would not be safe. He gestured and called for Terri and Yanni to come to him, but they did not notice him.

The wind rose to a shriek and blew out the campfire. Embers blew sideways with strands of smoke blowing before them. Everything loose fell over and rolled. Yanni lost his balance in the howl, recovered and leaped face first into Terri's chest. She threw both arms around him before falling over. Faringway was already in a vehicle. Storm sirens screamed miles away in Marfa.

The night clouds blew by in belts as fast as high-speed photography. Sand grains and raindrops struck Roller's face and hands like hot needles. Clouds streamed over in sheets no different from the campfire smoke. The tails of tornadoes spun out of the bottoms of clouds, twisting and kinking and rising back up or lengthening downward to strike the ground explosively. Higher, thicker ochre clouds rolled by as though the earth and all its dust was sucked up to blend with the indigo of night. Lightning strobed continuously, flashing jagged networks of light through the clouds and daggering the ground with murderous intent. Turbulence roiled in all directions, and the ground shook. Great hexagon slabs of cloud broke off in the clouds to pinwheel away, reflecting mirror images of the sky and earth. Curiosity overcame fear, and Roller watched, clutching the side of a vehicle. Then a cactus needle speared his chin like a dart. The smell of blood took over as Roller dropped and pulled the needle out of his face.

Faringway slammed the door of Roller's SUV closed and kept his head down. Terri and Yanni huddled in Faringway's vehicle while Laney Joe gripped the roots of brush clumps growing in the small gully he'd crawled into earlier. Even so, the wind flattened the woody branches over his head and shoulders. He feared the wind would pull the brush out by the roots.

The earth buckled, and Marfa's storm sirens ceased, replaced by the groaning of the mountains. Roller turned his head to see a line of white magmatic fire exploding along the line of the peaks to the east, and at last, fear reached deep into his gut.

Although they were miles away from the viewing station for the Marfa Lights, suddenly the atmosphere was filled with a burst of them—globes of grayish light, dull red bodies, and clouds of tiny incandescent pin lights flying about at random at high speeds, leaving streamer trails behind them. It was as though someone had thrown a torch into a footlocker full of fireworks.

Everything in human vision quaked and pulsed as the volcanic smoke spread over everything, reducing the night sky to final, starless blackness. Roller wanted to change the channel. Objects from other worlds and times flew through the fog. *A hallucination?* There was a grand piano, a ballroom chandelier tinkling audibly and shedding glass, something that looked like a submarine, a McCormick reaper, a steamship, six bronze cannons, machines with flickering lights trailing power cables, paper, stone, autos, a locomotive, many utterly shapeless things, and human beings with limp arms and legs ragdolling through the atmosphere. The grip of time was broken, and bits of it all flew through this incomprehensible event. Roller hid his face.

This was so much more than a storm—earthquake, sky quake, reality quake. Fragments of everything breaking apart and blowing into a junk heap in outer space wailed in their desperation as they disintegrated. All love, fear, pain, hope, ambition, and longing swirled together in steam, blasted up the volcanic throats of the mountains, and launched into upper blackness.

Roaring static came from above, through the night and its few visible stars. Cracks speared through the view—not jagged, but immense lines, glowing and flying through the atmosphere and the sky like falling stained glass. The shard-like edges cut through the earth like teeth through cake, exploding lines and dust behind them as they sliced. Everything broke apart, and Roller's vision distorted like looking into a fun house mirror in an earthquake.

Roller could still see Alan Silvy's dark running figure in the desert. A shard line flew near and grazed him. Alan fell, one of his lower legs flung aside. The lines of splitting reality ran everywhere through furious panes of glass. A line ran between Roller and Terri and Yanni. The view through the panes was dim, but they seemed unharmed on the other side. Roller could not see Laney Joe anywhere. Another sharp line sliced with a metallic scream through the engine compartment of Faringway's SUV. The compartments formed by these monstrous panes of sky, space, or whatever they were gradually filled with dust, smoke, and a darkness so black even God couldn't see through it. Roller's last thought was to keep thinking.

5

A raging sandstorm blew away toward the Red Sea, leaving the landscape revealed as though a curtain had drawn back. Hexagon clouds dissolved beneath a relentless Egyptian sun. Ochre and tan sandstone cliffs retreated upward, bank upon bank, on either side of a desert valley. The air behind a few retreating dust swirls settled clearly and silently. The odd clicking sometimes heard in deeper silences gradually gave way to the buzzing of insects digging out from the storm. It felt like it was late morning, just as the cool of the day begins to dissipate and start its upward climb toward the heat of midday.

Laney Joe lay flat upon the desert floor like a dust creature. His disorientation was so complete he didn't care where he was. Something inside told him he was alive and should open his eyes. He did not try to stand up. He rolled from side to side looking at strangeness, content to stay low. Everything came back after a while, but Marfa, the storm, and even Terri were puzzle pieces that couldn't quite fit together. He lay spread-eagled like a hungover drunk spinning in bed. The universe spins; so did Laney Joe. *It goes on and on, and nobody knows if it returns to a place called home.* He lay back flat and tried to rest just a little.

Eventually, he heard thumps and bumps far away, and lying on his side, he could see a village in the narrow valley in the defile between the cliffs. A few dust clouds, smoke columns, or possibly cooking fires rose into the air. He saw columns carved into the rock in the cliffs behind the village. That drew his keen attention. He shaded his eyes and squinted. There were etched hieroglyphics between the columns—picture-symbols he could not read and a very tall bas-relief of a king-like figure. With his minimal education, he could not remember any culture from history classes that used hieroglyphics.

He fell back in the sand and dirt, overloaded. For the second time in five minutes, he gave up totally. He was as down and out as the times he lay inert on a cot in juvie, wondering what he had done this time and what was going to happen to him next. After a short time, he stopped caring. Having gone through all of that, the giant storm he had just come through was just another universal beatdown. *Probably not the last since I'm still alive*, he thought. He took his pulse with his thumb on his arm. *Yes, I'm alive.*

Eventually, growing thirst motivated him to stand and begin to walk toward the village. Staggering gave way to limping steps. With practice, limping gave way to jerky strides.

Around midday, he approached the mud brick settlement. By this time, he was walking very slowly with his hands held visor-like over his eyes and taking deliberate, lung-filling breaths. His energy was at low ebb, and he moved only by force of will. A small group of workmen returned to the village for the midday meal. They had reddish skin, black hair, and wore undyed linen kilts. Still, nothing about them revealed his location. Many tribal people wore linen kilts.

He made drinking gestures to them. One of the workmen gestured to him to join them. They walked in a line into the center of the small town, treating Laney Joe as if desert wanderers staggered to them regularly. They sat him in the shade of an awning. After he drank a few ceramic cups of water, they handed him a bowl of foamy beer. He almost fainted after the first long, cold, delicious draught. The nearby workmen tittered and smirked as his eyes rolled.

The mother of one of the workmen gave him a bowl of pasty, thick lentils with a large green onion in the side of the bowl. The other workmen used the stalks of their onions to scoop lentil paste into their mouths. *This is the food of the gods,* thought depleted Laney Joe, whose fiery breath the rest of the day was a constant reminder of lunch. Just his luck to find this cuisine when he didn't know where he was.

He had fallen among a clan of rock tomb carvers. The work was constant and took years. Eventually, he found himself in a square-cut tunnel holding a rounded, hard stone ball which the supervisor just handed him. Laney Joe laughed. So this was the price of lunch! His new colleagues pounded their stone balls into the end of the tunnel against the limestone face. It was dusty and lit dimly by a single torch. He and the men all wore light linen masks over their faces and heads to repel the limestone dust. He assessed the workmen's work intuitively without knowing a word of their language. He engaged that little bump in his mind he called "knowing." He just knew how to do things—lots of things, complicated things. He entered the rotation of workers pounding at the stone face. He held up his end of the work.

Progress was measured in a few inches per day, monitored by a scribe. That person occasionally walked into the tunnel with a paper scroll after first having the carvers leave the tunnel so the dust could settle. Laney Joe saw a scribe assistant carrying an additional torch. The scribe sometimes made measurements with a knotted string and then carefully examined the architectural plan on the paper scroll. Work resumed when he left.

Laney Joe stole a glance at the open scroll before the two walked away. He saw more hieroglyphic markings on the paper. They looked like nothing he had ever seen.

Despite not speaking their language, Laney Joe appreciated the camaraderie of the workmen and even joined in with their work songs. As a result, he knew about ten words of their language by the end of the shift. He seemed to be naturally adaptive to new situations, and he knew he would gain a lot of solutions when he learned the local language. He threw himself into learning it.

At the end of the day, an exhausted Laney Joe was led to a room in one of the fired brick houses of the village, which one of the workmen told him was called Deir el-Medina.

Laney Joe's body wanted to drag him into sleep, but his mind insisted on pondering the nature of his arrival there. He missed Terri, Yanni, and Roller—Faringway, not as much. Silvy was such a cipher he was easy not to think about. Yanni was a special worry, though. Laney Joe felt he might have let down the boy by losing him. Where was Yanni? Where was Terri? Where was he? Where were all of them?

Without anything to grab onto mentally among all his impressions and memories, he gradually slipped into sleep.

In the days that followed, little things crept into memory. A growing seed was the peculiar impression that the people of the village had almost been expecting him, as though dust-covered strangers wandering through their village was a regular occurrence. With his limited vocabulary he engaged in a gesture conversation with the woman who brought him his food. "Where am I?" he asked. She put down his food, gestured to it, and gave him an appraising look with one eyebrow slightly cocked. Then she walked out of the room.

Laney Joe's life in the village lasted about thirty days. He talked to everyone to learn the language, and he made great progress. Among other results, he became the village favorite, its mascot. And then one morning, a few hours before sunrise, before the flight of the falcon of dawn, a glow of torches approached the room. A man jostled him awake. The man was bald and wearing the ubiquitous linen skirt. Laney Joe's eyes opened wide. The man made repeated gestures signaling Laney Joe to come with him. He was not unfriendly or threatening. Laney Joe managed to pull on a clean linen skirt left for him in the night, stand up, and walk out of the room. He laughed briefly. Life turned and turned again.

6

In her first waking breath Terri almost gagged. The humid air reached into her throat like a gulp of hot water and the air wrapped her body like a warm bath. Yanni was crying somewhere nearby. When she opened her eyes to search for him, she discovered she was on a low tree-covered rise.

Looking under and between branches, she saw the early morning sunrise mirrored at a distance by a few twists of a lowland river. Still, she looked for Yanni. The humidity cast a haze over everything in view. Yanni screamed and writhed about ten feet up in a thorn tree. Trying to climb down, he had hit a ball of thorns. He was pulling them out and crying when Terri rushed up. She picked him out of the last branches, then started thorn removal and brushing away of tears.

"Where are we?" he cried. Children always asked the toughest questions.

The spines gave Yanni some slight swelling, but his innate child's resilience and immune system kept him conscious and uncomplaining while Terri pulled out the tiny needles.

Once the job was done, they wandered in search of water. They walked slowly through a lowland rainforest. Terri held Yanni's hand and assisted him as the fever and swelling he had gained from the spines subsided. They were completely mystified as to how they'd gotten there. She could not answer his questions. The high, triple-canopy trees were loud with the calls and chatter of animals, and they found some pulpy fruit under a feeding attack by birds and primates. Leaves floated down to a carpet of tropical forest duff and a brush understory. They picked some low-hanging fruit in the tree branches that hadn't been sampled yet. They were as sweet and juicy as mangoes.

The way through the low brush seemed more open along the river. Dense brush and trees grew there, but there were also animal trails and open grassy strips. The two newcomers washed off, watching carefully for alligators, and drank from clear, flowing pools. They couldn't worry about bacteria in their thirsty state; they had no tools. Eventually, Yanni began to feel better and his curiosity returned. They made a game of spotting brightly colored macaws in the trees and following them visually when they flew.

The birds offered Terri a clue that she and Yanni were in Central or South America. She believed macaws were found only in the Americas, not Africa. She thought that trying to discover where they'd found themselves was a sweaty parlor game. The real mystery was how they'd gotten there. And above all, how could they get back? Would she ever see Laney Joe again? She deliberately stopped thinking about him.

The trail broadened and dipped slightly to a lower riverbank. The place looked to her like a landing place for launching and receiving boats. The landscape appeared maintained, which gave Terri some comfort that there might be human beings about.

Her speculations soon ended. As they paused to examine the open area, they heard people talking and perhaps approaching from farther down the trail where they had been walking. Soon, a group of men came toward them. They seemed to belong to a tribal group and were clad in woven fabric loincloths or skirts. Their skin was sunburned brownish-red. Their hair was black with trimmed bangs in front but various styles on the sides and in back—long, short, cut, or tied up with fabric scarves. She saw that one member of the party wore a masked headdress and a sash with designs on it, possibly hieroglyphs.

"Help us, help us!" shouted Terri and Yanni together, running to the group. The party of men recoiled, startled. Terri and Yanni stopped. Everyone stared at them as if they were an apparition.

The mask-and-headdress man, obviously the party leader, spoke in an unknown language and pointed with a club toward the landing spot. *What did he mean by that?* she wondered. Walk in that direction? Yes, probably so. But first the leader walked up to Terri and touched her cheek. The party relaxed at that and continued to the landing spot. Terri got over her fear of being touched, knowing she didn't have much power in the situation. She had never been political or manipulative of others, but she knew now that she would have to negotiate with the tribe for basics such as food. *Give to get.*

The party divided their attention between the river, Terri, and Yanni. A large raft of logs lashed together came into view upriver. A large number of people on the barge guided the craft, seemingly only with long wooden poles. An immense gray boulder sat amidships. *A raft transporting a boulder.* She found that very odd.

As soon as she saw it, she heard the unmistakable rhythms of chanted poetry coming from behind her. She turned and saw the priest chanting and gesturing in the direction of the barge. Voices on the barge returned the chant.

The group of men fell back from the priest reverentially, and Terri and Yanni followed suit. But a man near Terri gasped and ran around to face her. He stared at her feet, then screamed and fell back, holding two fingers in the air. The overwrought group, save the priest, fell onto the ground in worshipful poses.

Terri looked down. There, plain to see, were her ballet-deformed first and second toes on both feet. The two sets of toes were curved symmetrically inward toward each other. Her toes were a self-induced deformity that had also been a constant embarrassment in public when she went out with her feet exposed. Now this. She had left the world of professional ballet and was never going back, but she knew it had stamped its indelible mark in her mind and on her feet. She almost fainted, but she braced herself with her arm gently on Yanni's head. The group of tribal men stared at her toes in worship.

Yanni wrapped his hands around one of her legs, shoved his face against her belly, and cried.

7

Roller woke up slowly on rocks. He thrilled at being alive, but he knew instantly that the Marfa event had transported him somewhere else. The cold wind told him that. The stinging puncture wound of the cactus needle in his chin shouted a reminder of the event and proved the bizarre occurrence was not a dream.

He mapped plenty of pain elsewhere in his body as well. He stood up, trying to find his balance, and every movement was excruciating. He gained a small victory when he decided that nothing was broken.

He looked around to discover he was on a beach of smooth boulders, cobbles, and gravels. To one side shushed low waves against the boulder beach. Farther out, an almost motionless body of water—steel-blue and mist-shrouded—extended out of sight.

Roller scanned the inland direction. Flood channels filled with driftwood offered barriers to travel. Farther back, fir trees faced the beach. Farther still, the trees rose immense and deep in ranks, and their green shadows verged on black. *Shadows are the signposts to mystery,* Roller mused through the pain.

Roller could see the horizon in just a few places. A mountain range created a jagged line on the world's boundary. One mountaintop was obscured by a cloud. Roller took that to be a volcano showing some activity. Here was a sea, mountains, and a boreal forest. He stood up to view a high-latitude land far, far from Marfa or any land he had ever visited. His confusion was not alleviated by thinking about it. He was disoriented and it was getting worse with the new information coming in. He tried to think and take one step at a time. He thought it a miracle that he was still in his overcoat. He fastened it reflexively as a cold wind started blowing.

His immediate needs were food and shelter, but which way to go to find them? One way was as good as another. Catching fish with one's hands was harder than it looked in videos, but mussels and oysters didn't run very fast and could be eaten raw if there was no fire—if this was a local R month. He felt the nakedness of being a city boy in the wilderness. Still, the littoral beach zone was cold, windy, and wet—no shelter at all. On the other hand, the inland forest looked like bear country, so there he might be providing food rather than finding it.

Roller turned inland to gain more data. It was all he could do to deal with his indecision. *More facts, more facts.* He climbed down a bank of a gully, then up the opposite side. Then he worked through the sharp, broken branches of a fallen tree. He couldn't take much more without food.

He staggered into the forest, where the trees smelled sweet and piney. He heard birds singing but saw no signs of a bear. He watched his back trail, more to find his way back to the beach than in fear of predators who might be tracking him.

Hiking through the forest was definitely easier than along the beach. Fir and pine needles formed a soft carpet underfoot. He moved parallel to the beach so he wouldn't lose his basic geographic orientation. He walked inland just far enough so he could still hear an occasional wave splash out on the shore.

He saw a great fir tree with a skirt of fallen branches around it. He crept into the central space around the massive trunk, through the fallen limbs within the concealing, low-hanging living branches. He spotted a few strong branches growing out of the trunk within reach. Starting there, he visually mapped a climbing route up at least twenty feet. This gave Roller an escape route in the event of predator attack.

Returning to the dead branch skirt around the tree, Roller rearranged some of the branches to form a rough lean-to, and to serve as a barrier, with a narrow, open, winding trail inward toward the trunk for more protection. Then Roller ventured outward to gather a few armfuls of forest duff and brought it back to his makeshift camp by the forest giant. When his pine-and-fir-needle bed was arranged, he collapsed upon it.

———————————

Hours later, after some rest, Roller returned to the rocky beach to scoop through the tidal pools and light surf. He collected some mussels in freshwater pools. He opened the largest ones with lumpy shells using a pointed projection on a flint pebble—his oyster knife. The flesh, eaten raw, had a gritty, mouthful-of-sand texture. *Not an R month,* Roller mused. The flavor was of light seafood. He knew the sand was the developing mussel larvae malacologists called glochidia. The larvae formed in the flesh along with their incipient shells—the sandy grit particles—until they were expelled through the anal tube and pore in the miracle of molluscan birth. He spat the material, thereby killing thousands of future mollusks.

He found a smaller, smoother shellfish as well. He cleaned a handful of them in a clear pool. After a few minutes, they each protruded their foot, the organ which allowed them a slight degree of locomotion in the aquatic environment. The protruding organ was wondrous to Roller. The tip of the narrow mass was deep indigo, almost black. The color trended toward purple, fading to clear, gelatinous flesh near the shell edge. It was all shiny and wet. Roller bit off the feet and ate them without opening the shells. No sandy larvae.

As the sun set into the sea, Roller returned to his tree camp. He had seen no sign of human beings or bears. Two hours after retiring, he vomited and endured a violent bout of diarrhea. He ran a low fever. Roller was outside the shelter most of the episode so as not to soil his nest. He searched for and found a broad-leaf herb that served well for cleanup. *Try to avoid the indigo mussels,* he told himself.

Groggy, feverish, and with blurry vision, Roller worked his way back into his tree nest holding the branches for balance and support. He still had a few cogent thoughts. The most important one was that the downwind odor signature of his camp was probably that of a three-week camp instead of a one-day camp. His waste was signaling predators of all sizes of his diet and state of health. He was outside the life he had known, and vulnerable or not, he fell into a reverie.

His thought path began with his memory of a very clear epiphany, an inner vision that came to him when he was standing in a field as a boy. He sensed the sky as a giant bowl overturned above him. He stood on the flat earth, in the center of everything, under the zenith, with the strong feeling of being drawn upward into the sky. He knew that his life must remain here, joyously, in the center and as a part of everything. His curiosity would investigate every buzzing creature, flower, and lordly tree that arched upward and every furry beast that ran over the surface. He didn't know the name of it then, but his education would drive him along a road straight to wildlife biology. The experience came back now from his deepest mind, perhaps as a way of reminding him that he had gotten himself into this predicament and he had no one else to blame. But he felt no blame or shame, only a curious exultation. Adventure had found him in a world almost beyond all knowing.

He had blown past a few opportunities for relationships and marriage in the effort to rush out to the fields and forests. His friendships were many, but formal and not close. A lover not long before had been the exception, but she had simply disappeared from his life. Mahan Faringway, the computer programmer, stood out by way of antagonism, a necessary colleague at the engineering company where Roller gained postdoctoral employment. Faringway also taught at a community college; thus as a professor, he seemed to feel that he could provide commentary about things of which he knew nothing. Their debates were legendary. Looking back, he realized that Faringway probably shaped his adult intellect more than anyone else. And when it came to designing his mega-tablet, Faringway was a full partner and didn't ask to be a signatory on the patent applications. Part of that may have been Faringway's personality trait of criticizing every element of the design. Dealing with the fabricators of the prototype, the only copy in existence, was an easy stroll after Faringway.

The corporate terminations of Roller and Faringway—Roller had smuggled the mega-tablet out of the offices—threw them onto the path leading directly to the world-breaking storm. Everything else between the firings and the storm was inevitable. Naturally, Roller and Faringway would work together on independent contracts out of the bitterness poured over them like gall at their professional maltreatment. Faringway wanted to hurl something he considered stupid in the face of the corporate world—ghost hunting would work well, and so he threw himself into researching the paranormal and watching internet shows on the topic. Roller's anger was much cooler. He'd always had a nagging curiosity about the Marfa Lights, and he took his time to design the experiment, hire the team, and travel to Marfa and Terlingua. His commitment, set in concrete, was to conduct the most offbeat but meticulous science experiments unrestrained by corporate and university rigidity. Knowing his work would be falsely labeled pseudoscience meant nothing to him. He preferred the term alt-science. Gaining the grant from the Berkish

Foundation had been too easy, looking back at their grandstanding and drive for publicity. It was somehow, mysteriously, too easy, as though they had the fix in, but Roller didn't know who had done the fixing. And he was still vexed with how Don Berkish knew and disliked Faringway so much. Roller and Faringway were co-chief executive officers of their small company, splitting the grant money down the middle, although he knew Faringway had disputed that just before Marfa blew up.

With his fading strength and buzzing, spinning consciousness, Roller pulled himself from his thoughts and climbed his escape ladder of tree branches up to a safe height. He found a section protected by nearby branches and sat with his back to the trunk on the downwind side. He unbuckled his belt, passed it around a small branch near his waist, and re-buckled. Roller settled into his perch. Despite his discomfort, he felt light, almost floating. He fell asleep.

He dreamed he was flying, or rather, floating. He wasn't floating in darkness, however, but in clouds, their tops in sunlight. The faces of his team appeared to him—Faringway, Alan, Terri, Laney Joe, and that little brat Yanni. They yammered and talked, with the exception of Alan. Alan's face flickered like a low-wattage hologram. The team members' faces were bordered by soft, colored lights—blue mostly— but also yellow and brown. The dream became lucid, and he thought of the Marfa Lights as soul lights. He wondered if everyone was alive. *Alan, not likely,* he thought. Then the dream took control again, in neon strips, hexagon clouds, and fantastic landscapes. A new face with Asian features appeared. It was someone he did not know. A new cloud appeared and built quickly into a storm with objects flying out of it like the world-breaking storm at Marfa. The Asian face remained, coming closer and closer to Roller.

Hunger woke him in the gray dawn. His arms and legs were asleep and his back rigid. He worked his limbs for a solid ten minutes before he regained use of them. He unbuckled his belt and started his descent from the tree. It took him half an hour to reach the ground. He examined all points for predators lying in wait.

Roller walked to a section of the beach where he knew a small stream released fresh water into the ocean. He drank and washed briefly—the water was frigid—and began a search for mussels that wouldn't make him sick. He walked along the beach a short way and saw a low mound of fur topped by a conical hat made of reeds. The figure seemed to quiver, bobbing up and down slightly. Realizing it was a human being in a fur robe and cape, Roller ran forward shouting.

The robed and hatted figure stood up with a lidded basket. Streams of water which had just been swirled through the basket to clean its contents ran out of it. Roller ran up making food-to-mouth gestures, a universal gesture of hunger and request for food.

Then he stopped and looked. The face seemed very close to the face in his dream last night. The person nodded, looking at him with familiarity while holding up the lidded basket. She gazed at him more and more intently, either trying to break through his lack of understanding or to gain a response from him without saying anything. She removed the basket lid and showed him several indigo-footed mussels while knitting her brows and continuing to stare at him.

Suddenly a voice sounded clearly in his head. *Here, eat these.*

8

Mahan Faringway fell three feet onto soft, grassy turf with wild-flowers and low-growing cactus. Then he bounced over the edge of an angled gully bank and slid down the gravelly slope almost to the pool of water at the bottom. A big, round turtle drifted slowly away underwater.

Outraged, Faringway stood up at the muddy edge of the water and cursed and railed at fate without quite knowing at the moment what his fate was.

The sun beat down on a grassy landscape with belts of trees bordering the grassy meadows. Low, rounded hills stood above the trees, but the hills were scattered around at random. An elm mott crowned one of the gently sloped hills.

When Faringway found his balance, he reached around and pulled a small cactus ball out of his shirt back, cursing all the while. He stepped upstream along the bank until he found a clear pool of slightly flowing water. Satisfied that the water wasn't stagnant, he drank some and washed his face. The air was very hot and humid—not like Marfa.

At last, he took a good look around. He descended slowly into fear like an emotional puppy. He had no knowledge of his whereabouts except that this land was not the semi-arid Marfa plain. The heat drove him out of the streambed, up the bank, and across the meadow to a belt of trees. He still wore a hat but kept his hands up to shield his face. He spotted a tree with deep blue shade and crawled under its low hanging branches to the refuge of its trunk. It felt ten degrees cooler in the shade.

Faringway settled in with his back to the tree trunk. Gradually, he could think again, and as he calmed himself, he became obsessed with discovering his location. Images of the Marfa Lights and the vast storm blew through his mind. It was impossible to sort out everything he saw into any coherent pattern. Fearful again, he wrapped his arms around himself.

He looked out upon the sunny meadow beyond the shade. Everything looked aggressive and threatening. Faringway decided to stay in the shade and rest while waiting for ideas and solutions to present themselves in his mind. He slept. Images of the storm flashed behind his closed eyelids in the same fashion as the images of highway stripes and mile post signs after driving long distances.

Hours later, Faringway woke, oddly rested. In his sleep, he had relaxed until he was sprawling on his back with only his head propped up by the tree trunk. A few leaves had fallen on his chest. He crawled out from under the low tree branches until he could stand. He straightened his stiff back slowly and looked up.

The night was absolutely clear and full of stars. The Milky Way stretched its broad silver band across the zenith down to opposite horizons. Constellations familiar to Faringway shone brightly. Old friend Orion, with its belt of stars and nearby Pleiades, dominated the eastern sky. Sirius the dog star, the eye of Canis Major, chased loyally behind Orion. Cygnus the Swan soared in flight along the Milky Way and high above all care. To the north, Draco slithered around the pole, and the Great Bear, or the Wain, pointed to the North Star. It looked slightly off-line to him.

That settled it. He still stood on planet Earth. He chuckled drily. Moreover, he languished in the northern hemisphere. That cut the uncertainty in half but didn't give much comfort. Where was he exactly? His thoughts sped up. His exile was like a coding problem without a guiding computer language, or like trying to find a GPS waypoint without any satellites at all.

Faringway heard a clatter of hooves and watched a herd of deer run out of a belt of trees and trot along a meadow. They seemed to have no fear of him. Paying tribute to his scouting youth and his orienteering lessons, he struck out northward toward the pole star. The travel was easy under bright starlight and cooler than the day. He looked for signs of human beings.

The land lacked fences, trails, roads, and radio towers with aircraft clearance lights. No wind farms blotted out the sky. Another fear built in him. *When* was he?

Nocturnal wildlife seemed to rule the land. Family groups of raccoons milled around under the trees, crooning to each other. Coyotes howled eerily in the far distance. Individual animals rooted in the brush and grass. Faringway couldn't make out what they were, although once he detected a distinctly skunk-like odor. He jumped back in fear when he caused a flock of wild turkeys to take flight. Their huge wings boomed in the air as they beat heavily for altitude. A cock circled around to dive, pecking at him as he neared. He ducked and ran erratically a short distance, and the turkey flew off to rejoin his mates.

He made little progress, but it didn't matter as he had no destination. All he knew was that he was nowhere near Marfa in space or time. The growing realization was a hard sell in his scientific mind, but he was learning to accept reality as it came to him, not as he had constructed it in computer labs. Oddly, his pursuit of paranormal phenomena offered good preparation for this situation. Except that this setting, both familiar and bizarre, lay beyond anything he had anticipated of the paranormal.

He continued walking until he became tired. Loneliness set in. He missed his colleagues and was surprised how much they had come to mean to him so quickly. He found another tree for protection and, after checking around it for prior residents, curled up at the base of the trunk and slept.

He woke to the sun just having risen. He resumed his aimless trek, only this time hungrier. He did not go far before humanity found him. He had advanced across a flat river flood plain and saw a line of people ahead of him walking at an angle to his line of march. He broke into a run to catch up with them. He dodged around a bush just as a long stick seemed to fly by where he had been running. Aggressive whoops and calls came from behind, and Faringway twisted around to see two loincloth-clad men running after him and closing in. Frightened, Faringway ran faster toward the group of people, but soon became winded, slowed to a stop, and raised his hands in the universal "I surrender" gesture.

The two warriors ran up. One had retrieved the stick thrown at Faringway. It was a lance, thicker than a mere stick, and tipped with stone flaked to deadly sharpness. Faringway had accidentally dodged death.

The warriors continued their aggressive shouts and gestures, slapping and shoving Faringway as the line of people he had seen rushed up in a group. The warriors prepared to spear their lances into Faringway's stomach and make quick work of him. Then, an odd figure quickly ran up shouting and set himself between the warriors and Faringway, who was immobilized by fear and certain he was going to die. The man who ran up wore a headdress of deer antlers. He had white painted zigzag lines running down his chest with white circles between and outside the painted lines and down his legs. He wore a loincloth like the rest of the group. Faringway, fearful as he was, understood clearly that the man had authority in the group.

But perhaps the chiefly figure did not have enough authority because the warriors turned their ire and shouted at him. A loud argument ensued in a language Faringway had never heard before. The antlered man remonstrated with the warriors not to murder Faringway, who had managed to take a breath. The authority figure made several gestures toward two men at a distance from the group. They had been carrying a large bundle wrapped with a deerskin. The antlered man seemed to be telling the warriors and the group that murdering the strangely dressed foreigner was unseemly at a solemn time like this. The warriors eventually backed off, frowning and glaring at Faringway. Faringway surmised that the warriors were the security guards for the group. He also knew that warriors in hunter-gatherer groups such as this one killed outsiders to gain prestige within the group. The antlered man had shown his power in denying the warriors their prize. A feeling of gratitude washed over Faringway, although he knew there was still an element of danger in his presence in the group. The antlered man gestured curtly for Faringway and all the group to return with him on their line of march. As Faringway joined the march and neared the men who bore the bundle, he realized the deerskin wrappings contained a body, and he had joined a funeral procession. He marched along with the joy that it wasn't his.

9

Laney Joe walked over a sandy expanse, through palm trees, and into a narrow passageway between huge stone blocks, the perimeter wall of the temple precinct. This was the back-door access of the complex that Laney Joe was allowed to use. The carved stone pylon of the temple lay far to the front, past a maze of sanctums, courtyards, and living quarters. Laney Joe thought of the architecture as more complex than the maze of grammar of the language he was steadily learning. He had discovered in himself a facility for languages he didn't know he had. He was far more familiar with the language than the architecture, although his experience with the tomb carvers in Deir el-Medina gave him an emerging appreciation for the massive stonework. It was clear to him now that he was in ancient Egypt. This realization was from his memories of the few picture and history books he'd been given access to as a boy.

He entered one of the scribes' rooms. The vast changes brought on by the world-wrecking storm at Marfa were only now being felt in him after a few months. The thought of Marfa, however, led to the thought of Terri's face, and he knew that the longings of his heart could not be dissipated by any storm or any bizarre flinging backward across time. *Take it as it comes,* he told himself for perhaps the one-hundredth time.

He was surprised to see the priest Khan-ep in the scribes' work room. Khan-ep was the one who had come to Laney Joe in the pre-dawn darkness at the village to bring him to this temple.

"Greetings," Khan-ep began formally.

"Greetings," Laney Joe replied. After a few exchanges, Khan-ep expressed his satisfaction with Laney Joe's learning the language.

"I can tell you more now of how you came here," Khan-ep stated forthrightly. He gestured to some reed mats where they could relax. The scribes paid no attention to them and returned to their work writing on papyrus. Laney Joe sat cross-legged in the Egyptian fashion.

"The priests with whom I live have named you, Young Falcon," said Khan-ep, bowing slightly. Laney Joe bowed in return, not knowing what to say.

"This is not my home temple." Khan-ep went on, "I am a priest of Amon at the Temple of On in Heliopolis. The priests there have a special concern with the...ancient issues, those such as you seem to embody. When they hear of the arrival of a visitor, they send priests to investigate. That is why I came to you in Deir el-Medina.

"From time to time people—beings—appear in our land like the Horus falcon that flies at dawn. Thus, our priests call all such falcons. Only a few, such as you, learn our language. Others cannot learn it, or not well. Some are very strange indeed. We ask all village leaders to look for them and offer food when they find them. The villagers at Deir el-Medina liked you because you went to work stone carving with them. You seem to have talents beyond what you are aware of in yourself." Khan-ep paused to drink water from a small cup. A scribe poured water from a ceramic pitcher and hurriedly brought it to Laney Joe, as though he had forgotten his manners. Laney Joe nodded his thanks.

Khan-ep continued, "When communication is possible, we ask the falcons where they came from." Khan-ep shook his head slightly. "It is never the same place. For generations, it has never been the same place." At the word "generations," Laney Joe's heart sank.

"Most of the falcons do not know how they left their times and places and came here. They have no say in the matter. That is the same with you, is it not?" Khan-ep smiled slightly. "Of course, when there is no pattern, one reverts to one's own frame of reference. Our priests have decided that you all came from one or another place in the Zep-tepi, the First Time."

Laney Joe pricked up his ears. Here was new knowledge. Khan-ep picked up on his interest. "Zep-tepi was the time before the land you see here, the time within which our greatest monuments were built. We know little about it. Some think—"

And here words failed, and Laney Joe resolved to work harder on the language. Khan-ep laughed and shook his head, bringing the story to a close. "Regardless of the debate, we all agree that the falcons are calling cards from the Zep-tepi, each one a call to faith, and we honor you greatly."

Khan-ep bowed deeply in the sitting position and stood up, Laney Joe following suit, but he was not ready to end the conversation. He took several seconds to formulate a statement in his new emerging language. "Khan-ep, I am learning so much from you, but people in my time speak of your time as being in our past, not our future. If that is so, I cannot be from the Zep-tepi."

Khan-ep bowed deeply again. "I will say it another way. If time is cyclical, as we know it to be, then the Zep-tepi is before us as well as behind us. Others of the visitors have come from our future as well." The other priests in the room murmured their agreement.

"Will I ever return to my time, whenever it is?" he asked, his heart pounding.

Khan-ep's eyes flickered briefly before returning to Laney Joe's face. "It is possible. But the others we have found followed many pathways through this time-way. Some of them disappeared, possibly to return to their homes. But since they disappeared, how can we know? Others have sickened and died. Still others have stayed here and gone on to great things."

A rustle went through the room of scribes. They had started gossiping about the happenings of the visitors they knew about. Scribes, the journalists of the ancient world, were privy to many things. A few of them frowned at Khan-ep as though trying to shush him for revealing too much. Laney Joe was amused. Khan-ep raised his arms repeatedly for silence.

Khan-ep drew Laney Joe into a quieter corner. "Our priests want you, Young Falcon, to be a 'Watcher' to look for others of your kind who may appear. You may contact them, learn if they share your ways, and gain knowledge of benefit to you, and possibly to us, of course."

"I wouldn't know...where, or how, to look," stammered Laney Joe, choosing Egyptian words as well as he was able.

"Ah, but who better than one of the time visitors themselves?" Khan-ep continued, smiling. "We have discussed this much among ourselves. You see things apart, from the outside. We see only from within our own circle. Your view sees some things with greater clarity."

Khan-ep's logic was irrefutable. The occupation given him by the priests kept him in touch with the bizarre event that brought him here; it touched his mind and allowed him to keep part of his focus on Terri.

"We will leave here in a few days when we take care of other items of business," Khan-ep said. "The priests of On are anxious to meet Young Falcon."

Khan-ep and Laney Joe took their leave of each other, and Laney Joe strode out into the sands, a spy for the priests of On.

10

Terri and Yanni walked along the forest trail in the line of men. The surrounding trees opened out, and they saw in the middle distance a pyramid about one hundred feet high. The monument was truly imposing, and it sat in the middle of an immense courtyard. The ceremonial precinct lay enclosed by smaller pyramids and stone houses. Ceremonial procession-ways radiated from the central pyramid in the cardinal directions, through the courtyard and beyond. Village homes lay in the trees and fields all around. Hazy smoke from cooking fires rose like ribbons in the air. The sights were so unexpected in their vision, they caused Terri and Yanni to "ooh" and "ah" in wonder.

The smaller pyramids angled upward in immense steps to flat, wide terraces, then up again in the steep upper slopes of the stonework. Some of the pyramids rose to temples at the top, others merely to an open, high table.

The central pyramid was nothing like the others. From the high, narrow, tabletop at the apex downward, they could see that the slopes were fluted outward, their rounded surfaces widening toward the bottom to form the wide base of the monument. Seen from directly above, the pyramid appeared to be circular with a broadly scalloped edge. This provided a great contrast with the square and rectangular plans of the other pyramids and temples. Terri thought that if she could actually look at that monument from such an angle, it would look like a giant flower blossom dropped face down upon the earth, giving it an enormous kiss.

The group with Terri and Yanni approached the outer precincts. Terri felt like she was back in her dream before the storm. Yanni's eyes were wide open. Another group of men, and some women, walked hurriedly from within the ceremonial district. The men wore more elaborate skirts, sashes, and headdresses in diverse styles. The women adorned their bodies more plainly, wearing thong-like loincloths with no tops, save for multiple-gemstone necklaces, Terri noted with interest. The headgear seemed symbolic, probably heraldic, signifying membership in clans or castes. The women's headgear was simpler—bright fabric bands with carved shells to match the men's symbolic displays. The carved shells affixed to the headgear caught Terri's fashion-forward eye with their iridescent gleams. She was reminded of a poet who described the life of tribal people as one of artistic splendor.

Yanni couldn't take his eyes off the ear spools of carved jade in many of the men.

"How do—" he started.

"Shush," cautioned Terri. "We have to be on our best behavior."

The priest they had met by the river stepped in front of them, facing the priestly group, presenting Terri and Yanni to them. He stepped away and pointed emphatically to Terri's crab-claw toes, which were bleeding now from walking too far in flip-flops.

The group began talking excitedly and arguing among themselves. The drama could not squelch Yanni's boyhood curiosity about everything around him.

"Terri, I've seen pictures of pyramids like these in books. They're like Mexico. When are we going to eat?"

"Soon," she lied to reassure him, then caught herself. "Um, well, I don't really know about that, Yanni. Maybe some of these folks will help us out."

She was tired of putting up a brave front, hiding her fear from Yanni. And how was that protecting him, anyway? She wanted to let go and have a giant, satisfying wail, but she trapped the tears coming to her eyes, forcing them back inside.

Eventually, a small subgroup of similarly attired priestly types came forward, walking slowly. One of the women carried a water pitcher—at least it seemed like a water pitcher—and she poured the water on Terri's toes to clean them and take a good look at them. The rest of the priests bent over to look at them as well. The woman showed her a stone bowl containing a small amount of what appeared to be freshly ground herbal salve. Terri nodded, and the woman applied it all over her toes and feet. Her feet felt instantly refreshed with some slight tingling and a growing numbness, similar to Novocain.

After that, the group dispersed, and the tall, young chiefly aristocrat with eyes for Terri took them to a stone room in one of the platform pyramids lining the courtyard. Clearly, this priestly group had won the keeping rights for them. The women were far more interested in Yanni than in Terri, walking up and squeezing his arms and legs. Yanni's shyness kicked in, and he clung to her.

In the small, dark room, unadorned women carried in a large pot of water for cleaning, another for drinking, more fabrics, and a couple of pairs of the loincloth strips.

It was obvious some people were higher and some were lower here. She was impressed with Yanni's guess that they were in lowland Old Mexico among the pyramid builders. Separation between the classes seemed to be a timeless concept. After all, somebody designed the pyramids then ordered others to build them. It had to have been like that everywhere. Terri made the universal sign for "let's eat," rubbing her stomach in a circular motion while gesturing the other hand repeatedly toward her open mouth. The young priest smiled and left the room immediately.

"Will we ever go home?" Yanni asked again.

"I don't know," she said, attempting strict honesty. "At the moment, I hope that we get some food."

It occurred to her that they were living in a vast teachable moment. Engaging him more, not less, would help them both. "Yanni, I'm honored that you ask me questions. Keep doing it; I need to know what you are thinking. I only feel bad that I have very few answers right now. I believe you're right that we're in Old Mexico with some kind of pyramid builders. You are a very astute observer. But the bigger question is, how did we get here? Probably if we ever answer that, we might get a few more answers on how to get home. For right now, I'm just glad that we got through the giant storm at Marfa and you are with me. How about you?"

Yanni looked at her and gave a giant grin that destroyed the tear tracks in the dust on his face. He grabbed her and hugged her hard, as a seven-year-old boy would.

Soon, they received some food. The young priest came back with a steaming stone cooking pot held in two hands and padded with folded fabrics. He set it on a stone bench and went outside.

Hungry as they were, the two newcomers approached the pot carefully and waited for the steaming to stop. Terri fished around in it with a clean stick. It was strips of boiled pumpkin. Three red peppers floated in the broth. She pulled those out and set them in a red line on the stone bench. Ten minutes later, they could hold the strips by the rind and nibble the flesh.

Yanni unwisely took a huge bite and gave his trademark scream. He spat pumpkin in a huge arc, throwing his head around. "Hot!" he cried, referencing the spice level. He ran to the water pitcher.

Terri took a more moderate bite and the fiery sensations seemed to take over and counteract the herbal Novocain in her feet and legs. She stepped to the doorway and gestured for anybody outside to come in.

It was the young priest. She led him to the stone bench and pointed to the line of three peppers there. She held up three fingers to the priest, then dropped two of the fingers, leaving one up. He laughed and left the room. Soon, a servant or slave came back with two fat, ripe mangoes.

11

Roller woke up in a mud hut after a good night's sleep. The indigo-footed mussels no longer made him sick. In fact, they launched him into a trance state with their hallucinogenic properties. The woman who'd greeted him via his mind was named Ah-noot, and this was her mud hut. She had already left the hut this morning. He reached for his pants, now dry after laundering in the stream outside. His overcoat aired out on a tree branch. The mussels seemed to produce a molecule in their flesh that built a bridge to some deeper part of his brain—the part with latent psychic powers. That's all he knew so far. His prior experience and learning gave him nothing else with which to understand this bizarre turn of events. He was beyond science now, and he tried not to fumble around too much in his brand-new basket of imponderables.

Crouching low, Roller duck-walked out of the circular hut's opening. He noticed the objects he'd had on him when the storm hit Marfa on a flat rock outside the opening, still there from when he prepared to wash his pants. The pocketknife, SUV and other keys on his keyring, and Faringway's EVP detector completed the inventory. His wallet must have been left in the SUV, wherever in the universe that was. The pocketknife was the only object of any use. Instinctively, he looked around for his mega-tablet. He knew it was gone, but now was the first time he felt lost rather than alone, completely hollow, like the Siberian wind was blowing through him.

Walking out for his morning routine, he passed the rack of drying pelts of arctic hares that Ah-noot had trapped. They were halfway between their yearly seasonal coat extremes, all with piebald patches of winter's snowy white and summer's forest camouflage browns and blacks. Roller grunted, looking at a calendar in fur. The fashion runway shows of Moscow and Milan would go insane over these pelts. Some of the prior owners of the pelts were already in Ah-noot's stone stew pot.

He stepped past a heavy wooden pole leaning against a tree branch. A large, stone clubhead was strapped securely to the top of the pole. It was Ah-noot's bear knocker. "Swing for the nose," was Ah-noot's only instruction.

When ready, Roller walked a long circuit through the forests and meadows, checking her hare-traps and resetting them when they had a hare in them. While carrying back one hare, he heard voices. A villager was excited. When Ah-noot saw Roller, she waved and walked off with the woman, carrying her bag of supplies on her back. He knew someone was sick in the village, and she was off to do her healing work.

Ah-noot was a mystery as well as a magnetic attraction to him. How did she make him telepathic? Or did he do that to himself with her only turning a few knobs and pushing a few buttons in his head? Talking in each other's heads was a form of deep intimacy, and Roller remained innocent of the protocols. He didn't know how to control his thoughts yet, but she did. He felt at a loss with her. He thought of fortune tellers at fairs with their turbans and full-length dresses with crescent moon and star prints. He was sharing a hut with a person like that, only stranger, more powerful, and kinder at the same time. And there was nowhere else to go where he wouldn't freeze overnight, perhaps even with his overcoat. Sleeping in that tree had been a risk. Ah-noot said he had done the right thing, but it was dangerous.

Ah-noot was the most generous person he had ever met. Yet, by the materialistic standards of his world, Ah-noot and her village society were poverty stricken and had almost nothing. He set to skinning the hare, spreading the pelt out on the drying rack and dressing the carcass for cooking. His steel knife eased the work considerably, although Ah-noot's flaked stone knives were wickedly sharp.

Roller knew from their knives and other stone tools that her world existed at a Neolithic level of culture set in a boreal forest. She was part of a mud-hut village society with no access to metal. They used stone-tipped arrows, clubs, and lances to hunt their food and fend off large predators and criminals. There were very few specialists in her world. She and other shamans were the essential but few skilled leaders available—a combination of doctor, priest, midwife, and university president.

They gained their knowledge from the trance world, but they shared it freely with their patients and others. The villagers didn't trust the shaman, even as they relied on him or her for help or rescue. The villagers didn't know where the shaman's knowledge came from. The mythology and folklore of witches probably arose from this mystery of ignorance and its handmaiden, fear. Roller knew murder of shamans had been recorded. Female shamans were rare. For these reasons, Ah-noot had built her hut far outside the village.

Roller remembered that early travelers in the age of exploration studied shamanism in Siberia, where the practice of shamanism was most pronounced. Later scholars noted that shamanism and its beliefs were found everywhere on Earth among tribal peoples, leading some to posit shamanism as the urreligion, or foundation of all religious practices among human beings. At least, the traces were there. The one thing that united and defined shamans was the access to the trance state and entry into the trance world.

A young brown bear had come by early that afternoon. Roller ran for the bear knocker while the animal watched his excitement dumbly. The bear seemed more inquisitive than aggressive, but Roller knew he couldn't take any chances, and he grabbed the bear knocker and attacked.

Roller ran just into club-swinging distance from the bear, took a wide, well-balanced stance and swung the long, heavy club as hard as he could. The bear dodged the first swing by sitting back on its haunches, still not aroused. Roller executed a few more side-to-side swings at the bear but did not advance his position. He shouted "Hey, hey, hey!" at the creature. His arms and shoulders ignited in soreness from the first swing of the club. He swung it a few more times at the bear and made aggressive noises at it. The bear, surprisingly flexible, twisted away from the danger zone to a safe distance, looked contemptuously at Roller for a few seconds, and left.

Ah-noot had a policy and protocols for bears. Young bears were the most dangerous. After they left their she-bear, they had great energy and set off exploring to carve out new territory. They had no experience and would happily move into Ah-noot's hut and eat all the flesh they found there. So, they must be driven off. Older bears were a different matter. If they showed up, they were hungry, but perhaps not aggressive. Ah-noot would throw them a large chunk of meat—a whole hare or two—and start a chant the bear would find annoying accompanied by rhythmic hand clapping. "Ut, ut, ut, ut…" All this was done while keeping the bear knocker handy. The goal was to make them leave and not mark the camp as a good place to find food in the future. Females with cubs almost never appeared. Human camps were far too risky places to visit with cubs.

Ah-noot had told him that once, many years ago, a bear had visited while she was deep in trance. She saw the bear clearly and made a strong telepathic connection. They visited, and the bear left, wishing her well. That was when the bears chose themselves as her totemic animal. One became her spirit familiar, her animal guide in the trance world.

Anthropologists of a more ecological bent always saw totemic animals as a species of high significance to the culture—either as food sources for hunters, predatory competitors, or spiritual guides. Roller thought for Ah-noot, bears were the latter. At least, she would never hunt or eat them or make robes of their hides.

The next day when Roller awoke, Ah-noot was up and about already, coming back from a stream with her mussel basket dripping and heavy. She sat down outside her hut and set out her ritual gear to prepare for a trance. She gestured insistently for Roller to sit in front of her, so he did. It seemed obvious Ah-noot wanted more serious communication with him than merely the gestures and rudimentary phrases he was learning of her language. Hence, magic mussels for breakfast.

The mussels were mild and good but no substitute for sausage, eggs, and OJ. Still, Roller was content to sit and gaze across the small stream to the solid, dense line of fir trees. Their branches waved in the morning's cool breeze. The wind sighed through the branches, which waved back and forth, back and forth, back and forth....

Ah-noot's voice announced itself in his mind. *I saw the young bear come to you yesterday,* she said. *Bears are special to me. I am sure it was not sent by an enemy in the trance world, but it is good to consider the possibilities. Yes? How could you have enemies yet?*

True, Roller replied. *I think the bear sent himself.*

They laughed. Ah-noot's eyes seemed to twinkle with lights of their own and crinkle around the edges. Her face was surrounded by a wide aura of Krishna blue.

But there is something about you and me and the ... she said. Here, the concept lay beyond telepathy even. Roller's psychic consciousness translated it as "trance sphere" or "world."

Ah-noot went on, *I know you are from my future because I have traveled there many times. I have gone many places in time.* She became thoughtful before continuing. *Not long before you came, I could not travel in time as before. It was cut off from me. Then, right before you arrived, I had a vision. Flying through the sky, I saw a large, thick arrow with a hard, bright flame coming from the back, pushing it forward.*

A missile. Roller immediately felt inferior to her. He had only seen her face in a dream walking along the beach.

Ah-noot ignored this unguarded thought that she heard clearly. *Then it flew on and time broke free again, and there you were. But I have detected in the trance world a very powerful, very unusual force that doesn't belong here. I can't explain it, but I know it is dangerous. It appeared quite a while before you came.*

This was almost too much for Roller. Here were the only clues to how he showed up in this place, and they came in the signs and symbols of a Neolithic shaman who had turned him into a psychic, or perhaps merely a drug addict. Ah-noot explained more about the trance world, sensing his confusion and the fear that comes with dealing with unknown things. And she was telling him it was dangerous. *Roller, I think of trance as a gateway into another world attached to Earth with its own vast energy, but still part of the planet. The world has many refractions. Trance just gets you to the gate. Once inside, it's the same world, but a variation of it in which you can fly and hear thoughts. There are certain differences that can guide you through. The six-sided figures, hexagons, are everywhere in the trance world; they are the building blocks of the trance world. I cannot explain them, but I work in their world for the benefits of far viewing and how thoughts are somehow unrestrained in this world. Herbs and medicines have no thoughts, only distinctive energies. I can find them more easily here and take them to another part of the world—the same world—where I need to use them. Things with great potential may not be explainable, but the potential is not to be overlooked.*

They floated in trance looking at the neighborhood and checking in on Ah-noot's patient in the village, who was doing much better today.

They returned to the hut and came out of trance, both drained of energy. They gradually came back to normalcy, and Roller tried hard to make sense of it all. Ah-noot finished the day sewing the dried hare pelts together, trying to make a garment.

12

Ah-noot flew far in the trance world without Roller. The unexplainable changes in this world required a deeper look, some kind of safeguarding review of this level above the human. Ah-noot knew of no enemies but was aware of evil spirits that wished ill on human souls, and the one she had mentioned to Roller was certainly one of those. Ah-noot knew the trance world started as a tiny point deep within her mind—the gateway—but then took her out of herself and into worlds far away.

Ah-noot's culture, like many prescientific societies worldwide, held what was called a three-level world view or cosmology. The solid Earth was the middle place where terrestrial life lived, breathed, and had its being. The Underworld was the domain of water, sea creatures, and oceanic deities. The Overworld was the vast province of the birds, the stars, and the higher deities. Ah-noot was grounded in her native cosmology because it allowed her to set things in order and identify many patterns on the Earth, the middle place. Ah-noot traveled the Overworld, the other levels as well, and points beyond all three in the trance world which touched, and perhaps tied together, all of them. She had to explore the driving questions, the unknowns in her cosmology, that had brought Roller to her and possibly less-personable and desirable entities as well. If the trance world intersected all three of the levels, it was only logical that it would have, or take on, qualities of all three levels and not all necessarily at once. She found this knowledge immensely empowering.

She visited all the places of unknown shape and purpose on the Earth known to her. She saw the milky, translucent corridors that came out of the far distance and encircled Earth. Some of them entered the ground, becoming dark tunnels with mouths that weren't visible on the natural surface. She suspected these of being of different timelines. Within them, she saw tiny soul lights firing, most likely conscious entities racing along some rollercoaster track of time. There were many of these, and she took heart at the crowded life of the planet, reveling in the companionship of sentient beings, welcoming them all. Ah-noot could travel different timelines if she chose well and left behind psychic breadcrumbs to allow her to find her way back out again. At the same time, she found she didn't need talismans for navigation as much as she had before, though other shamans had to have them.

She avoided alien entities, however, whenever she thought one or more traveled nearby. She noticed more of them lately, including the one who projected evil intent. She hid from that one and started to prepare defenses against it. Caution was essential when she couldn't possibly know its intent or potential purposes involving her. She knew Roller was an unwitting traveler in time, a castaway in the cosmos. He was different, but human, and deserving of her care.

Ah-noot chanted for her dim memories, memories of structures for which she could discern no purpose. Eventually, she found at least three—and she knew there were more—possible portals. They were apertures in the rock, tunnels, like vast caverns but without the translucent corridors entering and leaving them. It was as though they lay unused and forgotten.

She chose one of them and attempted to float her trance body into the mouth. As she descended, a sharp feeling of a sand grain struck her. Then several more hit her trance consciousness, just as though she were walking into a sandstorm. She moved lower and the intensity of the hits increased, like a river of particles flowing out of the cavern straight up into the atmosphere. No particles could be seen while she moved within their high-energy flow. Ah-noot removed herself from the pinprick river. Here were things she must study from afar, at least for now.

She moved away, remaining open to the new, distracting herself a few times to collect some lavender and eucalyptus from remote locales. She could collect things on Earth from the trance world. Roller called it psychokinesis, but to her it was just a natural thing for trance travelers. She navigated back to her mud hut home. She came out of trance easily, concentrating briefly on the earth on which her body sat. He was there, waiting for her. She smiled at him.

Roller could appreciate the relaxing effects of the two herbs, lavender and eucalyptus. He seemed so worried and in need of someone. For her part, it was a comforting thought to know someone was there at the camp. Having been alone for much of her life, the companionship and trust were sheer bonding pleasure.

She hurried to prepare the herbs for their many uses. Later, Ah-noot and Roller agreed that they were communicating more outside the realm of trance—spoken language, body language, moods. As usual, the more they talked, the more they fell into their favorite topic, the giant event at Marfa and its consequences. Ah-noot worked on her herbal preparations while they talked, filling her simple mud hut and hers and Roller's lives with healing and beautiful fragrances. Later that night, they made love and shared their sleeping furs.

13

The procession of loincloth-clad people and Faringway trod somberly through the grassy, wide floodplain until the midmorning sun grew hot. This was the most he had walked at any one time in his life. That and the adrenalized running he had just finished left him completely exhausted. He staggered, but the people around him scarcely breathed hard. Some chanted and sang softly while they walked. A low hill bulked above the flood plain ahead of them, and they made straight for it. They saw that the eminence lacked trees but was covered with scattered brush and patchy grasses. As they walked to the highest level, they saw soil disturbances where earlier graves had been dug.

Faringway fell into the reverential mood of the group. The friends and family of the deceased walked to a freshly dug pit and stood around it in a circle. Small groups of two or three individuals gathered at scattered hearths around the flat hilltop. Those folks were the gravediggers who had dug the new grave. They watched the proceedings quietly.

The two men with the hide-wrapped bundle stepped into the pit, not more than three feet deep, and lowered their burden. The antlered man chanted and slowly shook two rattles made of terrapin shells that were fastened together to contain handfuls of pebbles. As he did so, members of the funeral party came forward and placed offerings in the grave around the bundle. They placed a few large and well-shaped triangular stone spearheads, two tubular sandstone pipes with herbal material packed into the tubes, two pouches he later found out contained quartz crystals, and four thin sandstone grinding slabs with oval wear patterns. These were placed, one in each cardinal direction, to outline and frame the burial. A grieving woman came forward and held up her offerings: two large necklaces, each consisting of a hide strap fastened to either side of a large shell panel, the pendant of the necklace. The pendants were carved with intricate designs on their mother-of-pearl, bright iridescent faces. The woman arranged the necklaces on the bundle and stepped away. The deceased was a respected male in the community, kin of many in the social group. He was a person of some prestige. Faringway could tell from the richness and diversity of the gifts the people had placed in his grave.

A young man stepped forward holding an impressive antler rack in his hands. He set the antlers in place over the bundle to form a kind of cage arching protectively over the body. By this time, the antlered priest was chanting to the sky with his arms and face upward. He ended the prayer softly and lowered the rattles. He placed one of the rattles in the grave within the antler cage and returned the other to a pouch tied to his loincloth. The priest turned and walked down the hill. The mourners followed, forming a line again as they had when they had approached the burial ground. The grave diggers walked slowly to the pit with digging sticks and shell scoops to close the grave.

The mourners took Faringway to their encampment several miles away in the secluded woodland belts away from the river flood plain. The households were no more than sunshades of skins and hides strung between tree branches, or hides draped over saplings to form domed shelters, or wickiups. Groups of such shelters formed sleeping quarters oriented to central outdoor cooking hearths, which were simply pavements of stones with wood fires built directly on them.

At the edge of the encampment, the antlered priest stepped to the side and waved groups forward to their respective households, blessing them and putting an end to their mourning. The men with the stick lances returned to their families. The priest gestured for Faringway to follow him.

The antlered priest had only a single wickiup in his household, with two hearths several feet in front of the door opening. Clearly, he lived alone, but the wickiup was more substantially made with support poles and skins, and there seemed to be more room inside. The priest made a welcoming gesture to him, took off his antler headdress, and stepped inside his wickiup.

Faringway collapsed onto the grass outside. He was exhausted from walking for two days without eating or drinking, aside from the occasional sip from the numerous clear, flowing streams encountered on the march.

His fatigue told him he was alive, at the very least. It also proved to him that he was not dreaming. He had no doubt that the warriors' sharpened stone lance heads would have opened his guts in a gruesome, torturous death. He remained fearful.

The priest's offering to him of shelter and respite allowed the pressing questions to come flooding back to him. How did he get here? The question didn't stop presenting itself to him. And where was *here?* He knew the others from his group must be thinking the same thing if they survived the storm or event—whatever it was. And where were they? He seemed to have been thrown through time to a group of prehistoric Native Americans—an impossibility, yet here he was. And because he was alive, they might be alive also. That was a good thought, but it was only a point of logic, not observed fact. Their predicaments might be as dire as his or worse. He wanted to see them again. They had not been a close team, except for Roller and Faringway, but Faringway already felt the bonding from the shared, harsh experience of the Marfa event. It brought them together as a group of human beings but left them lost to each other. *Ironic.*

Despite the bizarre events, his mind and memory persisted in returning to the start of his life—his divorce—a hopelessly negative and embittering milestone. He could never seem to remember anything before it, and he punished all his colleagues at the engineering company, Alford Global, simply for being in his life at the time of the divorce. Naturally, they shunned him and demanded he get therapy, and naturally, he refused to get help just because they had given him that advice.

Faringway felt differently about Roller because Roller didn't engage. They became true colleagues over Roller's hobby mega-tablet. Roller tolerated his tirades and referred to them as "debates." At the end of the development period, Faringway felt redeemed to a degree, appreciated by Roller for his computational skills and ability to get work out of the fabricators. And at the end, Roller had a tough, field-worthy mega-tablet almost anyone could use with a set of qualities and functions that never would have occurred to Faringway. It had been a learning experience well outside the bubble of his perceptions and arrogance. He was grateful in a way he never could have admitted to Roller, but that was why he released all the patent potential—and there was a lot of it—to Roller. He marveled at how he and Roller had such a weird, complementary relationship—Faringway contentious and Roller always seeking harmony. It was weird but somehow codependent.

His fury rose to new heights when he, Roller, and a group of other talented minds were released from Alford. Faringway didn't want Roller to feel rudderless or unmoored, so he convinced him to start an independent research group. Most of all, he burned to find ways to punish Alford Global for its ingratitude when it had been he, Faringway, who had exposed Berkish Foundation's theft of materials and appropriation of Alford's software ownership. Much of the stolen work had been his programs. And even now, Berkish trashed him publicly for his doing the right thing by raising the alarm of the misappropriations. Alford did nothing. Berkish and Alford deserved each other. Still, he burned for justice with a side of revenge.

He knew that his hunger for vengeance could be satisfied in an independent group, gaining wealth and recognition in areas conventional engineering wouldn't touch. Playing ghost detector and researcher seemed like a good choice, if the many internet media shows about such activities were any indicator. It should be easy to hire young assistants who felt curiosity about the paranormal as well, especially in this world with its uncertain present and future. He was proven correct with Laney Joe and Terri.

He tried to get up from where he had collapsed and found himself painfully sore all over. He propped himself to a sitting position and stopped. He looked around for any angry spearmen glaring at him. He saw none but noticed how the households had no privacy. He could see right through several of the wickiups, and nobody seemed to take defensive measures around the encampment.

He turned toward the priest's wickiup. The priest was sitting inside with his face in his hands, weeping. Faringway started to turn away in respect, but the priest noticed his glance and gestured that it was a trifle. Startled at seeing a tribal chieftain and priest weeping, Faringway approached his benefactor gently. The man had saved his life and extended him the hospitality of his wickiup and fire hearth, and Faringway began to feel an obligation to him.

The man gestured for Faringway to sit, while he remained emotional. He made a sweeping gesture to all points outside, indicating his discomfort to be with his own people in the encampment. That began a long session of getting-to-know-you, gesture and sign language conversation. They learned the other's name by putting their hands on their chests and repeating their names aloud. The priest was Kheeg-ah-tah, and he learned Faringway's name as "Furrin-gwy." Faringway was amused and decided to go with it.

The language lessons proceeded from there. By chance, negation in both cultures was shaking the head, and nouns were isolated by pointing at objects and repeating the name. Kheeg-ah-tah began stirring and preparing a fire on the hearth. Faringway followed him around, practicing his new words and glancing around the encampment to see who was curious about the stranger.

Kheeg-ah-tah paused in his chores and began gesturing and speaking intently. There was unfinished business, and he needed to deal with it. Faringway followed his train of thought as well as he could through his exhaustion, interrupting Kheeg-ah-tah at points to clarify his meaning. Kheeg-ah-tah stopped in frustration and squinted shrewdly at Faringway, his unfamiliar clothing, and his strange metal gear, especially his pocket knife.

The gist of Kheeg-ah-tah's complaint and his crying was his people's ill treatment of Faringway the stranger. Kheeg-ah-tah lived primarily as a herbalist and healer, and he sought unity and harmony for all people in peace. Faringway fell back humbled and dismayed. He hadn't expected high humanistic values from anyone in such a low-energy, hunter-gatherer society. He had been saved by an enlightened soul trapped in a culture which sanctioned murder to heighten prestige. Faringway knew from his education that genius sorts out almost randomly through all cultures and all times by combination and recombination of DNA in genes, but sometimes a society may suppress the expression of any particular genius, because the society may be unprepared to receive his or her unique gifts. How any genius could emerge is miraculous. Perhaps Kheeg-ah-tah was one such genius, misunderstood and shipwrecked in time and in a way only slightly different from Faringway in his predicament.

Faringway knew that the principle of ahimsa, nonviolence, arose out of ancient Hinduism and was renewed in the twentieth century by Gandhi and Martin Luther King, Jr., both of whom showed powerful commitments to it and both of whom became martyrs to its cause. He wondered if Kheeg-ah-tah was a Gandhi or Rev. King in a different time and place yet running the same risks.

Faringway sank deeper into his fatigue after his intense effort to communicate with Kheeg-ah-tah. The last thing Kheeg-ah-tah conveyed to him before he slumped on the grass was to watch the encampment continually, that Faringway was not out of the woods yet. Faringway saw Kheeg-ah-tah give him another intense stare before walking into his wickiup as Faringway fell asleep on the ground.

When he woke up, it was the next day, and he was still on the grass, but there was a deerskin over him for a blanket. He hadn't had food in so long that he had lost his appetite.

Kheeg-ah-tah ran past him to the embers of the fire and built it up to reheat it. By the time Faringway had struggled into a sitting position, Kheeg-ah-tah had brought him some warmed-up meat on a flat rock. With the first bite, his appetite came rushing back, and the meat was gone in a matter of minutes. He pointed to the empty slab and made antler hands over his head. *Venison?* His cook shook his head and pointed to a charred turtle carapace tossed into the bushes. The meat was turtle, and it was delicious.

Kheeg-ah-tah stared intently at him yet again and pointed his finger straight up, then emphatically back at him, nodding his head. Faringway spread his hands and shook his head. He didn't know how he came here, and he couldn't explain his world with hand gestures. Still, the two men conversed briefly in sign language they made up on the spot. Oddly, Kheeg-ah-tah seemed somewhat satisfied with his answers.

Kheeg-ah-tah stood, stepped into the wickiup, and brought out a few pouches and one large, heavy deerskin bag. He looked around for a spot, chose one, and emptied the contents of the bag on it. The contents were dry, light tan sand. He flattened out the sand pile into a thin, even layer on open ground, and started to chant.

He lit a bundle of sage in the breakfast fire embers and smudged his entire household and Faringway, who knew enough not to interrupt a ritual. He cupped his hands and pulled the smoke over his head and body.

Kheeg-ah-tah took the smudge and chanted through the entire encampment. The other families ignored this as commonplace, no big deal, although some frowned at him and growled at him to keep his distance. He returned to the wickiup with additional tree branches and objects in his arms, the stub of the sage smudge still smoking where he had perched it on the armload of materials. He put the bundle down and stepped into the middle of the spread-out sand, still chanting—hypnotically, it seemed to Faringway.

Kheeg-ah-tah extended his arms straight out from his sides and pointed outward with his index fingers. He turned completely around, three hundred and sixty degrees, chanting loudly. He raised his arms directly over his head to point to the zenith. Then he stopped chanting and rotating, and he sat down in the sand. He reached over to one of his pouches and pulled out its contents. He brought out a stone bowl and three long spatulate objects.

The spatulate objects were each the same length, about a foot. They were no wider than three-quarters of an inch, and they tapered to rounded ends. They were made of exquisitely flaked golden brown chert stone and were extremely thin, translucent and a glowing caramel color when held up to the light. The edges were not sharp but had been ground smooth all around the perimeter of each piece. The stone worker who had made these items must have been a master craftsman. And they were gem-quality flint rock, very brittle and hard to work. He handed them back to Kheeg-ah-tah carefully.

Kheeg-ah-tah resumed chanting and installed the stone spatulae into the sand at three points around the circumference of a circle, angled inward toward the center to form the legs of a tripod. But their tips did not come together or touch. The shaman set the water bowl gently on the upper ends of the spatulae, completing the tripod and making sure the construction was stable. He poured water from a terrapin carapace bowl into the stone bowl atop the tripod.

He gazed far, far away as he knelt before the tripod. The sage smudge burned out and the smoke began to dissipate. Still he chanted while he held a sprig of cedar in one hand and stared fixedly into the water. Faringway felt his attention drawn to the water. Kheeg-ah-tah chanted softly while lowering the cedar sprig toward the still, silvery surface of the water. He chanted softly, then ceased chanting, and silence rushed in like the wave upon the shore. He touched the tip of the sprig to the surface of the water. Ripples flowed outward, outward, outward….

Faringway felt himself falling into the tiny pool of water, and at the same time expanding, becoming part of everything around him. Everything became clearer. He felt power and rose above the encampment as in a dream of flight. The world became crystal clear, his flight through it a kind of controlled ecstasy. He knew that Kheeg-ah-tah had taken him into a shamanic trance. Was this where he could find his lost companions? Kheeg-ah-tah flew nearby in the image as an alert, aware man. Kheeg-ah-tah's voice spoke directly in his mind, *So glad you could become a shaman. Now we can speak directly.*

Faringway recoiled in mild shock but not so great that he fell out of the trance. He no longer thought anything was impossible. Quite the reverse. Everything was possible.

14

The canoe with the priests, rowers, and Laney Joe took what would in future millennia be a vacation cruise down the Nile. The river here seemed about two miles wide, an ocean of fresh water flowing northward. The low banks on either side opened out on cultivated fields, palm and hardwood forests, towns, villages, and stone monuments. The empty deserts of hills, cliffs, and sand began less than a mile outward from either bank. The land, at least that near the river, looked as though it had been settled and peaceful for thousands of years.

The Gizeh plateau appeared above the left bank to the west. The shining white pyramids, clad in limestone and flanked by their temples and causeways, sat in calm magnificence atop the plateau. They were commanded and guarded by the jackal-headed sphinx facing the river and the sunrise. But they were not the canoe's destination, and they fell behind.

Downriver, the temple of On in Heliopolis had a dock and a modest causeway leading to its stone gateway. The temple itself was a hulking, mossbacked creature, with an air of antediluvian age. The corners of the building were huge, rounded and eroded limestone blocks like the shoulders of an old man collapsing into decrepitude.

Laney Joe had been invited by Khan-ep to attend a daily ceremony in the sanctum of the temple. Younger priests, townspeople, a few Hebrew servants, scribes, and students congregated in the courtyards and training rooms bordering the courtyard. Food vendors plied their trade under awnings propped up by poles along the dirt streets leading to Heliopolis town.

The ritual was very simple, almost like a church service. The priests led chants to Amon, the ram-headed god and others as well. Khan-ep stood beside Laney Joe whispering the chants to him so he could learn them. Other priests lit incense and flares on cue. The cult of On perpetuated Osirian religion, the dominant doctrine of ancient Egypt. The priests worshipped the creator god killed and dismembered by the evil Set. Osiris' wife Isis traveled widely in the ancient world to recover all his body parts. When she discovered them all, she sewed them together and wrapped them in winding cloth to make the first mummy. With additional divine help, Osiris was brought back to life. The hieroglyph for Osiris became forever and always a king wrapped in mummy strips. The powerful myth became the basis of the Osirian cult through thousands of years of pharaonic history.

The interior ceiling and walls of the temple were painted with scenes of ancient Egyptian history, framed and overlain with panels of stories in hieroglyphics. Laney Joe took it all in with awe. The limestone slab floor of the temple where worshippers stood—nobody sat in the ceremonies—was bare and sandal-worn save for four stelae spaced evenly along the central axis of the temple chamber. The stelae stood in narrow pyramid shapes about six feet in height. The surface panels of the pyramid stelae had hieroglyphic writing over every square inch on all four sides.

Khan-ep led Laney Joe out of the chamber when the daily ceremony came to a close and the incense began to clear. They walked through a low doorway into the inner sanctum behind the ceremonial chamber. The walls were covered with hieroglyphics from floor to ceiling. Khan-ep greeted a small group of priests there and presented Laney Joe to the group.

"Thank you for bringing Young Falcon down the river to see us," the leader of the group, a priest by the name of Thann-us, said. He was the chief priest of the temple and managed its affairs. He gestured to chairs and stools in the sanctum. They all sat.

"Finding Young Falcon wasn't the only business conducted on my trip," Khan-ep said with a wave of his hand. "I had to request our allotments directly from a few balky temples and grain managers. The pharaoh himself had to release our grain allotments with that letter I showed them."

"Who doesn't like us this year?" an aged priest in the corner asked.

"Probably the same corrupt officials, as always," replied Khan-ep. "Two more boats follow us with the allotment. We'll see how much of our foodstuff remains on the boats when they arrive. But it is always like this when the crops are short. Remember, the Nile flood was low this year. If it does not spread fertile mud from valley edge to valley edge, the grain planting is not as large."

Cynical chuckles were heard in the sanctum. A priest said, "Do you think this is why some scribes and accountants become richer than others? Think again." More laughter.

Thann-us raised his hand for order. "We all worship the same gods and nurture the same villages full of children. Yet we fall into disunity. These are dark days indeed."

"How neatly you bring the topic back to our pharaoh," another priest declared.

It was Khan-ep's turn to interrupt. "Please, let's not contribute to the disunity ourselves. Let Young Falcon wander Egypt but in useful directions." All gave full agreement to that proposal.

To the priests of On, Laney Joe was a surprisingly valuable find—one of the visitors who appeared in Egypt as if by magic. This was a perplexing situation, because none of the visitors with whom they could converse knew where they came from. There was always mistrust of foreigners, and if the priests could learn any patterns about the visitors' arrivals and departures from Egypt, then they could gain a degree of control over a very mysterious situation. Because Laney Joe was becoming a communicator, he might become a highly valuable asset, especially if he found and cultivated other visitors the priests might have missed. Armed with the priests' arts of divination, he might become more valuable still.

The priests peppered Laney Joe with questions. He tried to inform them with his limited but growing knowledge of Egyptian, but full communication would have to wait. The priests gradually drifted away, each one blessing Laney Joe as he left. Never in his life had that happened to Laney Joe, and he was staggered emotionally by it.

Khan-ep led Laney Joe to the corner where the old priest Lor-naat sat.

Lor-naat gestured for Laney Joe to sit. Khan-ep patted Laney Joe affectionately on the shoulder. "We all feel that you have it in you to learn our greatest ancient art. It is the trance world, handed down to us by the healing shamans from the beginning of the world. With it, you will observe and know all of the visitors. The learning is a blessing and a responsibility. Use it well." Khan-ep rose and left the room.

With flint and iron, Lor-naat struck a flame on a stick of tinder and soon lit a candle. He placed a bronze bowl with tripod feet on the mat and filled the bowl with water from a pitcher. He began singing about Osiris, Isis, Set, and Horus. The song settled on two lines of the lyrics, and the two lines became a chant.

Laney Joe joined in on the chant, repeating and repeating it. The candle flickered, and the tiny shadows inside the recessed carved hieroglyphs shivered. Soon the hieroglyphs themselves seemed to writhe and walk, especially the human figures. The horned snake and the long-legged stork moved in rhythm to the chant. The rising cobra swayed back and forth. The resting jackals flicked their pointed ears.

Laney Joe felt himself falling deeply into a meditative and profoundly hypnotic state. Was this the doorway into the trance world? The chant went on until, as if on cue, all the glyphs turned their facings into the stone, gazing into it deeply, compelling his eyes until he, too, gazed deeply into it. He gazed far, far in until he seemed to fall through the stone wall in trance.

15

Terri and Yanni ventured out into the steamy courtyard in their loin-cloths. Workmen were everywhere in the oppressive heat. Many artisans carved stone monuments at various locations around the ceremonial space. Carving was clearly the intention of the massive stone floated down the river days ago, but it had not yet been brought to the courtyard. Women hauled baskets of flowers and fruit to the finished monuments for their adornment and offerings. Gods of stone wore flowers and enjoyed fruit. Many of the women wore loincloths; some of higher rank wore sashes of brightly woven cloth. Other women were completely nude and carried burdens under the direction of the well-adorned women. Here was the answer to Terri's questions about slavery.

Terri turned away, catching her breath in the steam-bath atmosphere. This could not be her new reality, could it? She clutched Yanni, her only tangible test of reality. He was real, a boy, with as many fearful questions as Terri. They walked arm in arm, both with their chins and heads up, a flimsy front of courage as their only defense against the nightmarish horrors in which they found themselves.

They proceeded through their tour with an air of nobility that gained them much attention. They examined the stone monuments; most of them were colossal stone heads sitting directly on the ground in front of temples arrayed around the large ceremonial courtyard. The stone heads—gods, kings, or both—had fantastic carved headdresses with glyphs in various positions around the head. Several heads had strong African facial features; others showed Asian facial features. Most curiously of all, some of the heads, as well as some of the relief carvings on them, had European faces, notably with long pointed beards and headdresses resembling tricorn hats and conquistadors' helmets. It was as though the local people had received visitors from distant continents and had carved huge stone portrait sculptures to commemorate them. The diverse displays of imagery confused Terri further on exactly where in the timeline she had been dropped.

Her agile mind worked overtime to dispel the confusion. These were unusual human types carved into stone, and they seemed collected here in a time long before Christopher Columbus. Had they all been travelers thrown here by overpowering events similar to the ones she and Yanni experienced? They remembered only a giant storm with earthquakes, volcanic eruptions, and runaway lights, and they compared notes frequently on what they had experienced. But they'd seen no beings that seemed to be leading an attack. Was there some giant, cosmic puppet master behind the scenes pulling on strings and periodically setting beings down in this place? If so, why? Were her other friends and Laney Joe thrown into other places and times? Were they in some game, set on the board with nothing and expected to play? And the beings carved in stone, were they the game winners? Or the losers?

Terri chuckled softly to herself. Had she reinvented religion? Was this exactly like life? *We're born naked and helpless, and if we are lucky, we have a nurturing mother, perhaps a family, and after a while, we are set down on the gameboard of adulthood. Then we are expected to win a comfortable old age. Rules? You had to figure them out yourself.* Considering herself, Laney Joe, and Yanni, the thought didn't seem fair to any god she could recall.

Terri's main question was why they had not been set five-hundred feet down in an ocean or the same depth in the lava pool of a volcano. Their relatively gentle landing in lowland Mexico made her suspect that some conscious agency was at work. But she didn't have sufficient brain capacity at the moment to investigate it.

Other monuments held bas-relief and full-relief carvings on them. The flat tops of the monuments held offerings, and most of them were six feet or higher above the ground. The sides were covered in carvings of glyphs, mythic scenes, and seated gods staring out from caves carved deeply into the altar. One head-dressed god cradled a naked child where he sat. A few of the larger stone heads had pouty cleft-palette lips. Labrets closed the gaps. Terri noticed several of the priestly types wearing jade labrets in the same position as those on the stone heads.

While they strolled around the courtyard ever more reluctantly, Yanni caught his breath and turned to her.

"I just saw an Egyptian," he said.

"What? Where? Are you sure?" she said. "A carving on a monument?" Her reality testing collapsed, and Terri suddenly felt overloaded.

"No, no, a big man with a headdress like a snail shell. He was walking around. I've seen pictures of them."

"Okay, I'll keep a lookout for him, and we'll go over and visit if you see him again," Terri said, feeling more confused and lost than ever before.

The dominant motif of the carved altars was that of a snarling jaguar, clearly a major deity. Terri knew the jaguar reigned as a local forest predator from the pelts she saw worn as cloaks by some of the higher-ranking priests. Many of the jaguar carvings showed features of predatory birds such as eagles. Terri knew that combined animals were the idea behind the griffin in Greek mythology. Some fearsome monsters were a combination of a lion's body, wings of a hawk or eagle, and the venomous tail of the scorpion. Obviously, a cult of similar mythic beasts thrived here. Some of the stone heads depicted snarling jaguars with foot-long fangs, human ears, leather warriors' helmets, and name glyphs chipped into the heads as well.

In partial relief of this threatening atmosphere, small altars were built directly on the ground by families making pilgrimages to the temple center. They were usually framed by circles of slender statuettes of stone—abstract, long-headed figures standing at attention. The centers of the altars held small stone bowls of burned incense. The statuettes had long flowery garlands woven around and through them. Terri thought that the small altars were built in honor of family members who had died. The thought was a comfort, that these people at least honored their dead.

They walked on, Terri feeling increasingly like she was taking a child to an R-rated movie. Yanni became more nervous, walking stiff-legged and leaning into Terri for support. At last he broke, screaming again and pointing to a large altar. A jaguar's head stood in full relief in the side of the altar. In its wide-open jaws lay a carved stone child, obviously a young boy, alive but imprisoned behind its giant fangs.

Terri walked Yanni back to the small stone room as fast as she could, where they could feel some sense of safety, however minimal. Terri occupied Yanni with the basket of food the slaves brought by regularly. Later, the young priest, whose name was Cho-lub, came by and gave both of them a language session. They both were slow learners, but Cho-lub didn't seem to mind; he enjoyed spending time with them, especially Terri.

Days later, Cho-lub came by with a woven belt with long drawstrings for Terri. Terri saw immediately that the colors of fabric panels on the belt were red and a brilliant orange. These were the heraldic colors of

Cho-lub's lineage. Her belt told everyone she belonged to the lineage. Cho-lub handed a red and orange headband to Yanni.

Cho-lub told her earnestly that she was to be presented to the grand chief, in keeping with the ceremonial cycle that was turning. He repeated himself with numerous hand gestures, trying to explain the complexities of clan and chiefly politics that were probably far too complex for outsiders to understand, even if they knew Cho-lub's language. An upcoming ceremonial event was all she understood of it. Although she insisted that she and Yanni were not gods from the stars, she realized that by Cho-lub claiming them, his lineage gave them increased political prestige and divine status. It was not lost on her that it was to her advantage to leverage that idea for safety and privileges. She graciously accepted Cho-lub's hospitality. She could hardly reject it.

Nighttime came, and they attempted to sleep. She and Yanni set their pallets outside on ledges to catch any cool breeze which might blow. They started at midnight sometimes. Memories of Laney Joe came before any breeze, and she usually cried herself to sleep. Yanni felt even more helpless, but he pulled his pallet over and placed his hand on Terri's arm.

16

Roller strolled back and forth in a stream channel near the beach, looking for "pretty" mussels. He thought of Ah-noot and his new life as an unending dream. He wore a caribou cloak with a hood made by a villager. Ah-noot had bargained for it as payment for her treatment of her last patient, who was well and back with her family. This was healing from trance, yet another source of amazement for Roller. Did Ah-noot scry or read the entire universe from within her own head? Was it her imagination or did her head contain the starry objective universe? That would seem to be an impossible necessity to understand her clairvoyance and her unlocking of his telepathic ability. What was in and what was out?

Roller took more steps along the beach, and the fog made fantastic shapes among the fir trees and the hills inland as it rolled in from the sea. Where could Roller discover the key to finding his way back? *Tck... tck.* Back to where exactly? He wrapped himself tighter in Ah-noot's caribou cloak.

Ah-noot had put it together so far—the appearance of Roller and the cutoff of her time travel in trance. Was that universe in which she enjoyed such agency controlled by even more empowered agencies? From his perspective, that universe was unlocked for him by a molecule—a psychedelic substance in a mussel species. There had to be other keys, but while that universe's exploration was for him an ecstatic, visionary flight time after time, it also seemed framed and limited in ways neither he nor Ah-noot could explain.

He washed the few mussels in his basket and returned to Ah-noot's camp. When he drew near, he saw her outside the hut modeling her almost-finished rabbit fur robe, luxuriating in it and holding it together with her arms across her chest.

The Siberian winter was coming, and Ah-noot and the villagers were making preparations. Ah-noot declared a moratorium on Arctic hare trapping until their pelts turned completely white—perfect for high, fur top hats. Several carcasses had been smoked over embers and were hung in the rafters of the hut, and other masses of meat hung in the higher tree branches nearby. Any bears dislodged from their hibernation would be ravenous.

The hut needed to be fortified against them and the biting cold. Ah-noot wove rude mats from the leaves of a broadleaf aquatic grass species collected from several patches in the stream beds. Roller and Ah-noot worked the mats into weak parts of the hut walls and actual holes in the construction, covering them and fastening them in place with leather ties and sticks. Then, Roller spent a muddy day mixing mud pits near the stream bank. Together, he and Ah-noot applied a sealing layer of mud over the entire hut. At the top of the domed hut, they fashioned a smoke hole; the cooking-warming fire was directly underneath on a few rock slabs. Ah-noot handed Roller an eight-inch cylinder of bamboo. He wedged it into the other branches clustered at the apex and then applied mud all around it as a kind of mastic to hold it there. Smoke flowed gently through it.

Later, something occurred to Roller. *Ah-noot, bamboo doesn't grow this far north, at least not this well,* he asked her during trance.

Right. I brought it back from a trance journey to the far south, she answered. That was very clear to him, and the bamboo smoke hole made for a more comfortable hut. As the weather continued cooling, Roller brought in fuelwood to dry along the inside walls of the hut.

Their nights were warm, and they could now converse briefly without going into trance. Their lingo was English, Siberian Neolithic, and their own sign language. Roller wanted to know how she could travel in trance to specific places.

"I will myself there," she said.

"But what's the geography, the roadmap that guides you there?" he asked.

"I take a talisman, a token, of a person or something that reminds me of them," she said. "Sometimes the object leads me to the medicinal that helps that person. But I have discovered lately that I can travel specific places without a guide object."

"*Tck...tck.* How can it do that?" Roller asked incredulously.

"I don't know," Ah-noot replied in exasperation, "It just happens when I focus on it and see the image. Then I'll go to it. I can't explain it. We'll go together. I'll show you if you'll shut up about it."

Roller shut up about it. His line of questioning revealed to him what he really wanted—familiar faces. This Stone Age bizarreness had him barely hanging on. Ah-noot was his lifesaver. His only skill was slapping mud on the hut. He couldn't chip out stone spear points and was just barely learning to set hare traps with Ah-noot's repeated instruction. His mortality was as close as the next bear who could dodge the swing of the bear knocker. When Roller succeeded in trapping and capturing a small animal, he exulted and wanted to eat it raw. *Ha.* That struck at his thin veneer of civilization, leading him to speculate on the existence of some unexamined beast within—one that might be building up a head of steam to explode in a fugue of violence. Ah-noot had discovered psychic powers in him, why not some unspeakable Lovecraftian horror as well? *Whoa, boy,* he told himself. *Just cling to Ah-noot.* That thought had its charms.

But the tug of his old team was strong, and their faces were always with him. Laney Joe and Terri explored the depths of each other wherever they went, and Yanni tagged along. Yanni came out of nowhere. Faringway's intellect was rock hard, and Roller enjoyed chipping away at it, even when Faringway chipped back at him. Alan Silvy's mind had been an unexplored jungle, an Amazonia of anger and fear.

And now Ah-noot had suggested that he could communicate with them with a material item that belonged to them, the living ones, anyway. To Roller, that smacked of sympathetic magic and Vodun, which probably did have a few roots in shamanic trance. But Roller hadn't collected any of the team's nail clippings or hair swatches, and when he woke up here, he had almost nothing of his own, notably his mega-tablet.

That reminded him that he did have his knife, so he got up to step out of the overly warm hut and find his one remaining possession. Ah-noot used it most of the time now. There was starlight, enough to see objects ten feet away. *Where was Ah-noot working today?* He glanced around, checking the stone slab by the hut doorway where he usually plopped down the knife. He saw the black square that was Mahan Faringway's EVP recorder. Faringway had given it to Roller, but the object was still Faringway's in Roller's mind. Imaginative questions flooded Roller, some hopeful, some fearful. He picked up the recorder.

"Ah-noot!" he called with rising excitement.

17

It seemed like months went by, but Faringway could hardly tell without calendars or his cell phone. There was time in the transit of every day, and then it started over again, so time was cyclical. At least that was what his new people told him.

Kheeg-ah-tah had invited Faringway into the trance world so that he could communicate with him. Kheeg-ah-tah wanted to know where he had come from, and more deeply than that, what he could expect from him. Faringway related his information at length to Kheeg-ah-tah. The shaman knew nothing about substantial buildings, automobiles, roads, and houses that flew through the sky. However, in trance, he'd seen many boats on the ocean. Faringway readily deduced that there was a great differential in their original timelines.

Bizarrely, Kheeg-ah-tah knew all about the Marfa Lights. *Yes, they shine far away over the big mountains.* He gestured with his arm, pointing high and away. *They are the spirit lights of the ancestors. They come out to dance blessings upon their descendants and tell us all is well in the spirit world.*

So much for auto headlights captured in mirages, thought Faringway.

Kheeg-ah-tah was the shamanic healer for several local encampments and knew everyone in them. He had earned prestige among the people for his success as a healer and few accusations of witchcraft or trance medical malpractice. Those things were subject to change, however, and some greeted his skills with fear. How would the appearance of Faringway be treated by the community? Kheeg-ah-tah had learned the healing arts from his grandfather before him, including ritual ways of entering trance. The chipped stone spatulae for forming the tripod had come directly from his grandfather, but he did not know if his grandfather had made them.

Kheeg-ah-tah could see strangers in trance and traders who came regularly from the coast or from lands far away, but no individual as unusual as Faringway had ever shown up in Kheeg-ah-tah's land.

Faringway was astounded by his own sudden acquisition of psychic powers. He had direct mind-to-mind contact with Kheeg-ah-tah—the trait called telepathy and one known from folklore and a small amount of statistical research in Faringway's time. But he was finding that it was commonplace among ethnic shamans such as Kheeg-ah-tah. It was very strange, but it was more proof that knowledge was not the wholly owned property of the West. Faringway had prepared for his paranormal research with the team by studying many of the properties of psychic powers, clairvoyance, telepathy, and others. He found it all engaging, but its facts were obscured heavily by con artists, fraud, and sheer mendacity. The result for him was general skepticism but also motivation to pursue his ghost research and, of course, his drive to gain resources and notoriety. The outcome he had stumbled into here was wholly unexpected.

Faringway's time was divided now between the trance world and hunting and gathering. He felt an obligation to provide food to the generous Kheeg-ah-tah to justify sitting cross-legged on his turf and eating turtle. Beside turtle there was venison, squirrel and all the smaller ground animals. There were doves and quail taken by netting. There were pecans and cactus fruits and a cactus wine fermented in a hole in the ground and sipped with a long cane straw. Kheeg-ah-tah had all the recipes. Faringway brought back fuelwood whenever he found it. He also helped others collect the cactus fruits and dig their pits. Eventually, he started winning friends in the encampment by accident.

His life among the hunter-gatherers was occupying but did not relieve his despair from being lost in time. The "great breakup," as he'd come to call it, still fogged his mind. He realized he might never see colleagues, friends, and family again, not that he had many of those. He was lost in a perplexing and uncomfortable corner of time without any way to find his pathway back to his own world, even if the high-tech world had not been especially homelike to him. But it occurred to him that if he could actually move his body physically through the trance world—he had heard about psychokinesis, or telekinesis—then he might travel widely and look in on other times and places for his team members using a sort of psychic GIS system. He already could look in on encampments and recognize people, and Kheeg-ah-tah brought back handfuls of herbs and medicinals for his practice. Those materials were much lighter than a human being, but he decided to ask Kheeg-ah-tah about it.

While Faringway explored the land, Kheeg-ah-tah explored the trance world. He knew he belonged to it and that it was another level of the world cross-cutting all the others. That quality allowed him to travel speedily through all its levels. The telepathy and psychokinesis were parts of him only unlocked in the trance sphere. He didn't think much about the "how" of it. He also knew that his chants created and channeled his liminal state through the portal into that higher-middling-lower place. Then he exulted in the beauty of the trance sphere and his sense of flying effortlessly through it. Beyond that, he knew very little about that world beyond finding medicine to heal his people. He remained humble in the face of immensity, and he knew that was good. He knew that allies found there were very good, they taught him more and more about the larger world. And he also knew there were enemies that could harm him. Recently, he had sensed more of them in the trance world.

The appearance of Faringway, "Furrin-gwy," brought all the questions into sharper focus. The very strangeness of Faringway, his clothing, and his bafflement upon entering the homeland, convinced Kheeg-ah-tah that he had come in through the overworld but on an unknowing basis. He was certainly not an enemy but also not an ally who could teach them, given that Kheeg-ah-tah and the people were actively teaching him how to find food and all other necessities of life. However, the trance world showed some disturbance immediately after Faringway appeared. The hexagon shapes scattered around; those were the things that seemed to be building blocks. It was heart-warming that Furrin-gwy was such an enthusiastic learner. But where did he come from? Still, Kheeg-ah-tah believed he could teach him to become a good ally, and that was probably the blessing of Furrin-gwy showing up.

Some of the monuments that Kheeg-ah-tah knew and relied upon for navigation seemed disturbed, or adjusted in some way he could not quite discern. Mysterious areas appeared cloudy and dark. One particular presence was so dark that Kheeg-ah-tah knew it was a powerful, strange enemy. He gave that entity a wide berth. As a normally suspicious and cautious adult, he watched carefully for enemies and could see them before they saw him. But the trance world still had the exhilaration of flying widely on a clear day, unbounded by care. He flew in it, but he had to learn more.

Trance travel was one of Kheeg-ah-tah's few joys. As with most shamans, he had a degree of alienation from his society. His roomy, open wickiup was set apart from the other households of the encampment; his privacy was a screen of brush. As a young man, he'd had a few mates, but no children had come from them. They left, and one he remembered had babies with another. The open society, all of its members, knew he had less value as a man—no seed. His trance travel, his healing knowledge, and all his skills had an asterisk at the top of the list. He couldn't perpetuate the lineage. He could never be more than a second-class citizen, albeit one with honor. Kheeg-ah-tah sought his own path through the universe, perforce accepting the isolation.

In trance, Faringway observed a clump of sage and moved his consciousness near it. He focused on it and imagined it rising up. Kheeg-ah-tah had never thought about it much. It came up by the roots easily. He felt an energy tug and a slight decline in attention as he took possession of the clump. Faringway turned his attention to a small boulder and applied the same combination of energy and focus. He felt like he was being pulled into the rock. He concentrated more. The rock lifted a few inches and fell back down. Well, conservation of mass and energy held in the trance world as well, modified slightly by psychic energy. He was newly fatigued, but he'd still tested his hypothesis about psychokinesis and had gained a method for making use of it. He would improve with practice and maintain healthy energy levels.

Days and weeks passed, and Faringway continued exploring trance with Kheeg-ah-tah, who warned him to avoid enemies. As a precaution, Faringway chose a base away from Kheeg-ah-tah's wickiup and hearth in secret. After several sessions in trance, Faringway found he did not need the elaborate ritual Kheeg-ah-tah employed to initiate the ecstatic flight. Faringway's sacred place lay in a wide place on a deer path winding through a large cactus patch at a point shaded by two mesquite trees. Humans avoided the patch for obvious reasons, but Faringway could walk carefully along the deer path without getting stuck. Few knew about the path but the deer.

On one of his trance journeys, Faringway visited the Marfa Plain. The setting was idyllic, with vast meadows, grazing bison, and pronghorn antelope. The scene had an eerie quality for its lack of roads, fences, and power lines—none of the fixtures of modern times. It was definitely another time, but Faringway could detect light balls—of something— rising out of the ground and floating across the plain. Faringway laughed at the wave of nostalgia sweeping over him.

Faringway knew his discoveries and new skills would be tested soon because the mysterious presences were seen more frequently, as though they were looking for him or someone else nearby. The attack started after a long trance journey. Faringway sped back to his trance space in the cactus thicket. Kheeg-ah-tah flew in trance elsewhere, launched from his wickiup household. Not more than a mile from the encampment, a dark cloud, a presence, hovered near Earth. A strange figure, out of trance, stood under the cloud. It wore robes and a strange shell-like headdress. Five loincloth-clad spearmen stood before it. The odd grouping offered such strangeness that Faringway paused to observe their goings-on. Presently, the spearmen began waving their weapons and whooping. Faringway had heard those whoops before. The clothed figure pointed in the direction of Kheeg-ah-tah's encampment, looked around curiously at several points in the sky, and disappeared into the dark cloud—back into trance, it seemed to Faringway.

The loincloth spearmen ran screaming and shouting through the meadows and trees, no doubt a war party. Faringway, with his trance vision, assumed the worst. He tore through the trance world to the encampment, calling in his telepathic voice for Kheeg-ah-tah.

Kheeg-ah-tah's voice and consciousness came to him at once, "Yes, they have come to destroy my body, and yours, too, if they can find it. They have been sent by that evil presence. Such exist, and from time to time, they eliminate the healers. They come from a dark place."

"We have to stop them," said Faringway, expressing faith in his new powers.

"Not by violence. I decided that long ago. I'm afraid this is the end, at least for me. You may flee, and I say farewell."

The spearmen approached the encampment running. Children out gathering flowers and cactus fruit scattered and ran crying. Men ran for their weapons and older children and women grabbed clubs and rocks for throwing.

"No—we must survive this and resist," Faringway said forcefully. The two approached Kheeg-ah-tah's entranced body. A fine vapor of sage smoke hung in the air. War whoops could be heard on the far side of the encampment among the other families.

"Let's combine our efforts to raise your human body," Faringway said.

They came closer in trance. Faringway had told Kheeg-ah-tah what he was doing earlier, so both men in the trance world concentrated on Kheeg-ah-tah's body. It was surprisingly easier than expected with the two working in concert. They lifted Kheeg-ah-tah's body out of the concealing mist and moved it in the direction of Faringway's cactus hold. Faringway looked for the enemy warriors but didn't see any of them looking at the shaman's floating body. They moved him at low altitude to Faringway's trance place about two-hundred yards in the opposite direction from the attackers and set it down next to Faringway's body.

"Let's stay in trance until the attack is finished," said Kheeg-ah-tah. "Watch for the hostile presence."

They rose high and looked for the mysterious presence, but it had left the immediate area. The five loincloth spearmen sped away from the large encampment pursued by Kheeg-ah-tah's friends pounding them with clubs, jabbing at them with long sticks, whipping them with deerskins, and hitting them with fists if they were in range. Children threw rocks as the enemy ran away. This time, Kheeg-ah-tah did not weep at the violence of his people.

The trance world could be foggy and cloudy or focal and very, very clear. Kheeg-ah-tah and Faringway looked at the encampment. But far off in a fog, they noticed two figures approaching, gradually taking on clearer outlines as focus sharpened. Kheeg-ah-tah and Faringway refrained from returning to the camp. The faces of the figures became clear and almost familiar, surrounded by wide auras.

"Hello, Faringway," Roller said. Faringway's EVP was in his hand, and there was a laughing Asian face beside him.

18

"Young Falcon, come out of it," said the old priest Lor-naat, impatiently watching Laney Joe trying to snap out of his disorientation from his trance.

"You see the problem," Lor-naat said, heedless of Laney Joe's discomfort. "We can witness the grandeur of Amarna—the pharaoh's palace and temples—but we cannot actually see inside the throne room to view the person of Akhenaton."

"Eh, ummm," Laney Joe managed.

Lor-naat took that as understanding agreement. "That would not be a problem—he is such a distant and other-directed pharaoh—except for the potential harm to the country. We must see inside his throne room and private areas to learn his plans and the directions he wants to go. Obviously, the empire is falling apart, and our leader just sits on his throne and demands to be worshipped as the only god. How insulting. But what is the nugget of his rulership? Whither Egypt? The temples for all the gods contribute to the power and sovereignty of the pharaoh. We create of Egypt, this middle place, a match to all the gods of the universe. As above, so below. Can one pharaoh tamper with the planets and stars in their courses? I think not."

"But the tribute dwindles to nothing as managers drain it off into their coffers," Lor-naat continued. "Or else, the tribute is not sent to us at all in defiance. And believe me, the Army demands its pay. Still, Akhenaton merely assigns more work to the goldsmiths and jewelers, or so it looks. We need independent observations."

"And then there is the issue of the eternal god. Akhenaton has set up his entire reign, palaces, temples, you name it, to the worship of one god, Aton. Who cares? Our universe has many gods, and all may be worshipped to facilitate their nurture of the world. But Akhenaton suppresses all religious worship other than that of Aton—all of it, right down to prayers at family backyard altars. Most of it we ignore, as you have seen here. But Akhenaton is suspicious, as all pharaohs must be, that all the temples with their estates and priesthoods are arrayed against him, trying to undermine him."

"We are not undermining him, but we must remain aware of his potential for harm. We must watch him and the other temples in a spirit of self-protection. The temple of Set, in particular, would like to work harm anywhere in Egypt and blame it on us or some other convenient temple."

Khan-ep stepped into the small room and smiled at them. "It is time to host you at the food sellers," he said to Laney Joe. To Lor-naat he said, "How did it go?"

"It has barely begun," Lor-naat said as Khan-ep and Laney Joe left.

"Lor-naat has learned much in his ancient ways," Khan-ep said as he steered Laney Joe out of the temple grounds. "All self-centered and all-powerful pharaohs are capable of reckless endangerment of Egypt, but Akhenaton especially so. He has set up his monotheism, belief in one god, as nothing more than worship of himself. You see, the Aton, the divine sun god, stands behind the pharaoh. Aton must be worshipped, but only through the pharaoh, through Akhenaton, the sun god on Earth. Akhenaton stands in front of the idol and the people face him, praising Akhenaton. That's what Akhenaton wants; that's all he wants. That makes him prey for all the mischief-makers in Egypt.

"Lor-naat has discovered much with his strange, strange divination. He can also discover visitors such as yourself, Young Falcon, but within limits. He believes Akhenaton is a visitor, too, or a reincarnated soul, of the last emperor of Atlantis. He's not sure which."

"Atlantis!" Laney Joe's head was spinning again.

"Perplexing, isn't it?" Khan-ep asked casually. "We all know its history. It is written in hieroglyphics on the four stelae in the middle of our temple. You can read the glyphs anytime when you learn the writing. At the end of Atlantis, the entire civilization had fallen into corruption and hedonism. Its ruler was the supreme model of self-love, unwilling to listen to anything about the world outside himself, and he uncaringly allowed his land to fall beneath the waves, although some say the Atlanteans all left the world somehow. Akhenaton fits the model of the last emperor exactly."

"We have contrived a tribute-bearing shipment of grain and goods to the court at Amarna, a quiet peace-offering so to speak, to allay Akhenaton's suspicions for a while. It is a rich gift and will be well received. We will also present you to the pharaoh as a new young priest, making sure your hair is trimmed in priestly bangs. It is good that your hair is naturally black. Akhenaton is generous, especially if visiting priests praise Aton, and we will strive to have you receive a small gift from Akhenaton when you are presented to him, from his hand to yours, even the smallest token of regard. That will make it a talisman and signature of Akhenaton's energy. That is what Lor-naat wants."

"My god, that sounds like a lot of effort for a token," Laney Joe said.

Khan-ep laughed. "Indeed, it is. But never underestimate the deviousness of priests."

The Fractured Universe

Weeks later, four boats loaded with cargo, priests, and paddlers pulled up to the river dock near Amarna. When the cargo was unloaded, paddlers became bearers for the march to Pharaoh Akhenaton's royal palace. Messengers sent ahead weeks ago had come back with permission to approach the court. The party from On entered the large courtyard, broke out the bundles, and organized them into a processional march. The gifts were complete with heavy bags of grain and pitchers of oil and imported wine. Small chests of precious materials—gems, spices, incense, and gold—were borne by the priests themselves. Foot traffic in the courtyard and court was heavy; this was a day for many presentations from other temples, officials, and potentates.

Laney Joe followed Thann-us, chief priest of On, who led the procession, with Khan-ep and the others close behind. The procession included a lot of starting and stopping, and the formalism of the event taxed everyone's stamina. After what seemed like hours, they could actually see Akhenaton and Queen Nefertiti. The pharaoh was paunchy and unhealthy looking, just as his statuary depicted. Nefertiti, in her forties, was a beauty out of all time. She seemed to radiate an aura of intense beauty. Akhenaton's facial features seemed distorted and sagging, and he looked tired, but then they all looked and felt tired. Laney Joe was energized in spite of it. He was standing in the presence of a historical figure.

Then the delegation from On stood in the front; everyone put down their burdens and prostrated themselves before the pharaoh. They raised their cupped hands to Pharaoh and the sun disc carved into the wall behind him with its rays emanating from it. Each ray ended in a tiny, cupped hand. A few of the cupped hands dangled the *ankh* glyph, symbolizing life. The delegation rose then and the pharaoh and Thann-us spoke.

Thann-us turned and gestured Laney Joe forward. Laney Joe bowed again to Akhenaton, deeply. Akhenaton made formal greeting, speaking without any enthusiasm. Laney Joe held his cupped hands together, opening them when he stood. "A boon I ask, a memory of this day to live with me forever?"

At that, Akhenaton gave a more genuine smile, turned, and looked around his throne and effects, like a middle-aged man looking for his reading glasses. In that moment, Laney Joe saw that Akhenaton was "playing pharaoh." That small gesture showed Laney Joe that Akhenaton was indeed a visitor, not a palace child born to the throne. For his part, Akhenaton didn't act like Laney Joe was anyone special.

The pharaoh turned back and placed a heavy object about the size of Laney Joe's hand in his cupped palms. The presentation was over, they moved on, but Laney Joe sensed another outlying presence—another set of eyes on him. By glancing around, he placed that new set of eyes quickly. Yes, another pair of dark eyes with thick eyebrows on a heavyset man just outside the colonnade were fixed on him. Khan-ep followed Laney Joe's glances, then gave a body gesture to move forward.

The pharaoh's chamberlain directed the grain bearers to the granaries, the precious chests to the vaults, and the prepared foods to the kitchens. The day at Amarna was as difficult and as simple as that.

Laney Joe didn't look at the gift until they were back at the boats waiting for everyone to return. It was a golden pectoral, the central ornament of a large necklace. The goldwork was a cloisonné of a court scene depicting the pharaoh and queen with inlays of enamel, turquoise, and carnelian. The golden background showed the throne room wall with its sun disc and cupped-hand rays of life, and toy ankhs were strewn about in the goldwork.

"I hope this is good enough for Lor-naat," Laney Joe said. The priests and bearers laughed. They started the journey downriver to Heliopolis immediately.

Laney Joe turned to Khan-ep. "That heavyset man outside the colonnade was also a visitor. And he glared at me like he knows about me."

"This explains much," Khan-ep replied. "He is Horemheb, General of the Armies for Akhenaton. Of course, that only means he is loyal to himself; he is a powerful and dangerous force in Egypt today. He can make trouble or even destroy any temple group if they threaten him. He is best fighting Egypt's enemies outside the country."

"Why doesn't he stay there if that is his strength?" Laney Joe asked.

"He grew tired of the slaughter, no doubt. He was invincible, according to his soldiers. He would maneuver until the opposing armies were drawn up in ranks against each other. Then Horemheb would stand in the center of the line, raise his arms, and seem merely to point at the enemy ranks, some say while holding a short black cylinder. Then a wide gap would appear in the center of the enemy ranks where all the soldiers had screamed, flung around, and fallen dead. That was the signal for the Egyptian chariots to charge through the gap. They would home in on the palanquin and banners of the enemy leader and hack the poor unfortunate to small bits with their mighty khopesh swords. No living Hittite, Syrian, or Nubian will attack Egypt while Horemheb lives."

The nighttime Nile with its swooping night birds, gently hissing waves, and overarching stars offered its own world of beauty, but it was lost on Laney Joe and Khan-ep. They sensed the threat of Horemheb and the many dangers he and his faction presented to them, most notably, that he was a powerful visitor with unknown weapons and malicious intent. Laney Joe felt the thrill of intrigue and the fear of the unknown. Laney Joe and Khan-ep took comfort only in the river's cloaking darkness as the rowers harmonized a workmen's chant and rowed them unerringly to Heliopolis.

The bejeweled golden pectoral was good enough for Lor-naat. He ceased his preparations and gazed rapturously at the treasure for a few minutes the first time he saw it. He had spent weeks preparing for a trance viewing inside of Akhenaton's court close enough to hear the pharaoh, especially his blatant plans to suppress the temples. Lor-naat's priority, however, was treatment of the sick of Heliopolis. He was one of several priests who practiced ritual and herbal healing.

Laney Joe spent the time learning about the trance world with flying trips around Egypt but with warnings from Lor-naat not to view Amarna. Laney Joe was best at entering the portal after entering meditative trance, but he was shaky at navigating the bright overworld of trance, and he became fearful from time to time at the idea of getting lost there. At last, the time for viewing Amarna came. Lor-naat and Laney Joe sat close to each other in the small temple room, cross-legged, each lightly touching the golden pectoral talisman from Akhenaton. They chanted and entered trance expertly.

Amarna came into view quickly. It was not a court day, and the courtyards held few people. The courtroom, the same room in which Laney Joe had been presented to Akhenaton, came into clear view. Their viewpoint seemed to rest in a second-story corner of the high-ceilinged room, looking down on the throne and the people surrounding it.

Akhenaton conferred with his counselors, chamberlain, and the fearsome Horemheb, wearing his general's shell-like crown. Akhenaton was not at all well and leaned limply into the arms of the throne. Horemheb was making an earnest presentation, to which the pharaoh and everyone else only made gestures of negation. Laney Joe could not hear the statements of the pharaoh, or of Horemheb. The arguments grew heated in a babble of many voices. Nefertiti showed the unrestrained distress of a queen and made a sweeping gesture toward the entrance and the outer courts.

Nobody disobeyed the queen. The courtiers, with the exception of Horemheb, turned toward the entrance to file out while servants, the chamberlain, and Nefertiti faced Akhenaton to assist him toward the private entrance and quarters. Horemheb took a small object from his robes and pointed it at Akhenaton. The pharaoh, just having stood up, shouted, writhed briefly, and fell dead. A trickle of foam oozed from his mouth.

The servants made a pile around him. Horemheb looked around in alarm, sniffing the air as though searching for a scent in the atmosphere. Then he looked directly at Laney Joe and Lor-naat and seemed to growl.

Young Falcon, out! shouted Lor-naat.

A loud snap filled the temple room, and Lor-naat fell back, grimacing, and then fell to the stone floor limp and dead as Laney Joe watched, still halfway in trance and surrounded by sizzling, buzzing air. He saw shifting images before him, moving like the colors in a film of oil on a street puddle. He was content just to stare, as in the moments after a fully loaded wasp sting, when the pain subsides and a dreamy numbness takes over on the verge of anaphylactic shock. Horemheb had missed Laney Joe but hit Lor-naat.

His natural resilience took over, and he took deep breaths, but he continued to stare. He tried to think of nothing, but of course his imprisonment in time and his current mortal predicament, for which he was unprepared, took over and pressed down on him insistently. Preparation? He had never aspired to accomplish anything lasting in life, so no preparation necessary. He always ran from any authority who might have disciplined him—parents, teachers, cops, and judges—to achieve anything. *Run, baby, run.* He'd only ever run toward the playground drug dealer. Now looking at Lor-Naat dead, he felt the loss of his last possible guide, someone who could share a vision of the future with him. He thought of Faringway and Roller as men bound up strictly in their own warped minds, preoccupied and unaware of him. Terri was his best connection, and she shined in his life as an art-in-flesh wholeness who never needed him for anything, really. In that moment, he released her to her unknown section of time, wherever and whenever that was, and memories of her flowed down his face in a torrent.

In his defeat, all he wanted now was Everyman's Egypt. Life outside the temple was good enough for Laney Joe. Now he understood the visitors who disappeared into the desert. Laney Joe wanted only the Egypt of lentil paste, onions, and the occasional slow gazelle. Everything was loss; he watched the viscous line of blood creeping out of Lor-naat's left nostril. There lay his soul, draining into sand.

19

Horemheb strolled in a meadow of flowers. To his right, a wetland of papyrus with many blooming fronds flanked the wide Nile. Waterfowl rustled the leaves and fronds and squeaked and quacked. Insects flew from flower to flower. It was all gorgeous, and Horemheb thought he might go over and make dead a few ducks and take them to the kitchens for food tonight. A large bee with a golden metallic sheen from antennae to stinger rose up behind Horemheb and buzzed toward him. It landed stinger-first on his neck. The bee's machinery pumped the entire message into Horemheb's body before he could slap the robo-creature away to fall with its gears, processors, and flywheels spinning into the grass.

The message scrolled through his field of vision in electric pink phosphene letters. "Return to Thonlus immediately. Your mission in question. Other Houses demand report."

Horemheb bellowed. The nearby ducks and cranes took wing in a cacophony of alarm calls. Just when he was isolating promising solution paths, he had to go home. Horemheb stamped his feet like a child when told to come in for dinner.

This is such a beautiful planet, in spite of its dreadful political state, he thought with regret. This biosphere hung in the balance, and the Thonlusians had not yet secured it from the other vicious contestants. As he thought more coherently about the issue, he realized that this was a good moment to report back: he had just dispatched a group of soldiers to pillage the temple of On in Heliopolis. He had recently discovered that a brief record of Atlantis was recorded on the stelae in the central chamber of the temple there. The return of the soldiers and the turmoil after his dealing with Akhenaton would take time to play out to his advantage, and that was before he could read the stelae. He ordered the soldiers to pry the stelae out of the stone floor without obscuring a single glyph and bring them back to him at Thebes. Perhaps the soldiers would capture those odd viewers of him when he killed Akhenaton at Amarna. He'd thought he was the only visitor in the local fabric, but, of course, who could know such things for sure? He could not predict when visitors would show up. He turned toward the transport network. The star cultures operated hidden transport facilities on all of the planets with which they maintained contact. They contained hardware that boosted an individual's trance energy for interstellar psychokinetic travel. Horemheb had requested and received such a facility for location in Egypt.

Thonlus, Horemheb's home planet, belonged to a grouping of planet systems of star-traveling sentients, and it was hard to describe their political organization—whether confederation, empire, tribal alliance, or warring factions. The grouping had rules—oh yes, it had rules—and adjudged violators of those rules tended to have the surfaces of their home planets beveled flat. No single planet knew all the rules, but all the participants tried very, very hard to follow along.

If that weren't enough complication, there was a higher order level of sentient organization above the local group of planets. The Aat and their harsh critics across the galaxy, the Rrrl', were truly godlike beings. The location and nature of their life and its origins remained unknown to the local scientists, and inquiries into them were strictly controlled. Control was what it was all about with the Aat; they talked to the Thonlusians and others and informed them that they were under their control, but few knew what that control amounted to. On thousands of biospheres, as they referred to inhabited planets, no sentient had any awareness of the Aat or the nature of their control over the planetary culture. Clearly, the Aat believed in the light touch. Those who knew of the Aat, including the Thonlusians, feared them and would not challenge them. Horemheb had hitched his wagon to the Aat's star, and beyond that he didn't think about it much.

The rule makers in the planet group made a few rules to govern telepathic cultures, to give equity to the nontelepathic cultures. The runaway evolutionary advantage of the telepaths over their peers needed superorganic control at the level of stellar cultures. It was probably the one equitable accomplishment of the planet group. Approximately forty percent of the member planets were telepathic.

Horemheb pushed open the twenty-foot platinum doors of his House's modest hold on Thonlus, the House of Meno, and nodded to the seven-foot guards inside. The effect of the doors never failed to intimidate. The guards were dressed plainly in black, according to the clan's policies. A certain war a few hundred years ago set stringent conventions and standards for showing and using weapons. Now, concealment was of the essence. The psychic centers in the guards' ganglia had been excised before birth to heighten the security of their future employers. But that meant that as courtesy to them, all communication in the house had to be verbal. Horemheb made his way to his mother's chambers.

Lun, Horemheb's mother, got to the point immediately. They did not touch or give signs of affection. He knew he was in for serious business because her elevator throne stood at its highest position. Her jaunty blonde curls bobbed at the top of the column. There were no children in the room.

"The Phirlotians, Gonnlutus, and especially the Bik, are jealous of us for the license to seek the sharing rights to Earth," she said.

"All of them?" he said. "That leaves no other sentients on Thonlus."

"Don't make fun at a time like this," she said. "The other Houses pass their gossip straight up to the Aat—anything to undermine us. Of course, they don't know and aren't going to know that the evil Atlanteans have placed certain bans on the planet and left them in place while Atlantis collapsed in on itself. Why didn't the Aat destroy Atlantis when it had the chance?"

"Maybe because they were protected by the Rrrl'? There is good news—" Horemheb started.

"Such a lovely planet," Lun went on to herself, ignoring him. "It used to have an energy geyser. Running down now, I understand. And this diamond came from Earth." She held out a gem the size of her fist and pondered it. Tiny diamond sparkles fell out of her shoulders.

"The perfect combination of life-filled oceans and life-filled continents," she said. "We can change it all or leave it be." She wore queenly brocades and concealed automatic weapons and small black devices under her skirts.

She looked directly at Horemheb. "There are plenty of human sentients. You can kill all you want for your own purposes, but you cannot drive them extinct. That came down from the Aat. I suggest you get on with your mission, play out your Egyptian hobby, and someday, maybe you'll tire of killing sentients to watch their souls flit away like fireflies on a summer night."

"Oh, but the souls of the Hittite infantry were spectacular," Horemheb said without irony.

"You are a beast!" Lun screeched, gripping her throne arms. A guard peered in from a hidden door. "I'm ashamed for having you!"

Horemheb felt his brave front crumbling, but Lun sensed his discomfiture, and softened. "You can still please the Aat. Succeed as their steward, receive their wealth and rewards, and you will move up in the clan. Your father is so high in it now that he couldn't possibly care—but I do! Why are you torturing Egypt so much?" she asked.

"Sheer fascination for one thing," he said.

"Fascination with killing or some other reason?"

"No," he said quickly, "the whole mission—the Atlanteans' Hall of Records for one, is special. I know it is in Egypt because they have the only Earth culture that talks about Atlantis and has records of it."

Lun shrugged.

"And then there are the visitors."

"Yes," said Lun, seeming to gain interest.

"I think they blow out of the tunnels from different times and planets—for many different reasons," he said.

"Am I going to have to tell you to investigate those tunnels?" she asked sardonically.

"No, no, wait," he said. "They're all locked up tight in various ways. They can't be seen outside the trance world. I think one of them leads to the Hall of Records. A tunnel near Deir el-Medina appears to have had expulsions of beings over many thousands of years. Why there? I don't know. Maybe the lock was defective when it was placed on the tunnel by the Atlanteans when they closed the Hall. But the visitors come out of a different tunnel from different worlds besides Earth timelines. Hundreds of years ago, a very large being came through. He resembled a hippopotamus, the scourge of the Nile, and communicated only by telepathy. He never found a way back to his world, but the Egyptians worshipped him as a god. He lived happily among them for three hundred years."

Lun laughed uproariously. "How sweet! I love those humans. I may have to put restrictions on you from killing so many of them."

Horemheb appreciated the minimal encouragement, but he had become suddenly confused about his plan. He thought it unduly complicated by the appearance of interfering trance travelers on Earth, the earthly shamans.

Earth was a confluence zone of many timelines, some leading to what the Aat hypothesized to be companion universes. Nobody was sure, but the theory had been around for generations. The Earth, its electrical fields, the powerful life force among all its life forms, the petroleum muck that glued its crust together, and its sheer interior heat vastly multiplied the energy the planet radiated, making it a giant induction coil and things of which the Thonlusians could only guess. Perhaps the Aat knew, and as usual, wouldn't tell anyone but their favorites. But all the energetic forces may have been what attracted the Atlanteans to the planet and allowed them to grow to dominance—they were energy vampires.

Following his thoughts, Lun said, "Truly, the earthly shamans can achieve great power, but thanks be, as humans they seem to want to apply their skills for healing and alleviating the life sufferings of others. I think it may be that peculiar mammalian trait called 'love.' Thanks be, we don't have it. They will never go far with it."

Horemheb added to her thoughts, "More of the trance-traveling shamans are appearing, most of them relatively weak. I have attempted alliances with some of the earthly shamans but have had to assassinate a few also. It may be that the latest set of appearances were talents broken free or awakened after an Atlantean ban was released.

Lun was curious. "What form of ban was it?"

"It was a kind of time mine," Horemheb said.

"Oh, like a mercury mine?" she said.

"No, like a hidden explosive device," he said. "You know they left several behind before they left. This one was far down the timeline, too.

It was emplaced below the old energy fountain you like so much. The humans may have triggered the event by accident."

"Oh!" Lun clenched her fists. "Enough. More of their evil jokes. Just like the Atlanteans. The fountain was so mysterious and attractive. It was just waiting for a human to sneeze into it. Humans are so stupid." She rolled her large eyes upward and to the side as though hiding a private memory from Horemheb. He could tell she was stressed and her blood pressure elevated because her delicate neck pulsed and the scale pattern under her skin stood out slightly in relief. More diamond sparkles fell from her neck.

Thonlusian females formed and grew tiny crystalline diamonds in the skin along the sides of their necks, shoulders, and arms. It was an offshoot of the biochemistry that formed organic reptilian scales under the skin. But it was a process in effect only in females. Diamonds were supposedly formed under great pressure and heat in the earth. Biochemists had done much research on what they called seed diamonds and still couldn't explain them, but there they were, sand-grain-sized and gem quality.

Horemheb went on gently, needing to give a full report. "Somehow, the Atlanteans managed to trigger a loosening of time with gravity that allowed great slices of the planet to float out of place in several time periods and lines. The tectonic and atmospheric disruptions were immense."

"The Atlanteans must still be giggling over it, wherever they are," Lun said, coming back to herself. She steepled her fingers. "Do you suppose the Atlanteans believe they are crafting the evolution of the planet with such self-centered hijinks? Human scientists found evidence of a great extinction in the Phanerozoic era, about 1.2 billion years before this last timeline, before there was life on the land. No word on what caused it. In the Permian period at the end of the Paleozoic era, an extinction killed 90 percent of the life on Earth. Cause unknown, although scientists were beginning to craft their all-purpose "cometary impact" excuse with that.

Others believe it was a giant hiccup in solar radiation, and that squares up with the Atlanteans' sense of humor. The dinosaur extinction event was an actual comet impact 65 million years ago. The Younger Dryas event more recently likely was an outer space snowball near-miss, but that doesn't mean the Atlanteans weren't involved. We could investigate all those events fully if the Aat gave us full sharing rights." Lun dropped her hands in her lap. Horemheb could see why the Aat frequently consulted with Lun on engineering projects.

"You are sure Akhenaton was a self-aware reincarnated Atlantean?" she asked coyly.

"Yes, and I couldn't kill him fast enough," said Horemheb. "I had to pick my way through the local politics before everything came together."

"Good," she said, "I've never said you were totally inept in your planning and execution. Now, listen. The one new element in your assignment is to find the one extremely powerful shaman we have detected in the somewhat mysterious Earth timelines. We detect its energy, seemingly poking around the mouths or gates of the alternate universe channels but never entering them. Earth shamans seek allies in the trance world; you may be able to meet and gain alliance with that one in that fashion. If you can't, well, handle it your own way."

"Who is it?" asked Horemheb.

"We don't know," she said, "It's just a powerful energy blip. An alliance or control of that one will solidify or clinch our bid for the Earth with the Aat, giving the overlordship to the Meno for thousands of years. Darling, succeed and your name will be engraved on the stela next to the Emperor's forever. Fail and you go back to the clan's vats. Your potential will be incorporated into my next birth pod. I'm already designing it. Can I tell the other Houses of your rapid progress?"

Horemheb thought he might like to see thirty or forty new brothers and sisters, but not if they incorporated his protein.

"Oh, and something about time," she added in afterthought, "We have vast reserves of time, but perhaps you don't. The Rrrl' on the other side of the galaxy from the Aat complain that the Aat exceed their share of galactic resources. It could get ugly. If there is another war, many thousands of biospheres will be destroyed. We all must gain a good position before destruction breaks out. It would become unwieldy if some of us were stuck in the middle of a planet-building process."

Horemheb wondered why she had told him that he was headed for the vats before the nova bombs started puncturing stars. Lun always shared the grief widely. Horemheb felt as though he were flung face first into the acid already. He would vastly prefer to unlock the Atlanteans' secrets, find his unknown competitor, and, of course, rule the Egyptians.

Horemheb walked away after being dismissed by his mother. Kenli, his spirit familiar, rushed out from somewhere to grasp his legs as he walked away. The creature's wordless telepathic songs soothed him. Kenli was a non-sentient creature from one of the earliest telepathic worlds, Melofron. Kenli had a humanoid pattern but an extra elbow and knee in each limb. Over geologic spans, telepathy had spread by evolution to some of the non-sentient animal species. Nobody knew why. But in the animals, they just made music, crooning presymbolic thoughts a telepath could "hear." Thonlusians loved them for pets and spirit familiars.

20

Terri decided to raise Yanni's spirits with a picnic lunch set out in the shade of one of the stone monuments. It commanded a low rise above the river to the north of the courtyard, temples, and pyramids. The river below meandered wide and muddy, and the banks held a number of long traders' canoes arriving at the ceremonial center or preparing for departure. They were tens of feet long, and both ends were the same. Bundles of goods wrapped in skins piled up amidships. There was no doubt considerable wealth flowed through this pyramid-building culture.

The priests and warriors placed no limits on Terri's and Yanni's wanderings, knowing they would only become lost if they attempted escape through the jungle.

The monument Terri had chosen for their picnic was an old one; a side of it was hollowed out deeply, and a full relief carving of a priest occupied the mouth of the small cave thus formed. Terri examined the monument and its carvings and glyphs carefully for any depictions of child sacrifice. Yanni was living in fear and needed the weight of it lifted from him, if Terri could help him at all. The carved priest was one of the figures who looked decidedly European, with a long, pointed nose and pointed beard. His headdress, however, was towering and blocky and covered with glyphs and symbols. It resembled a large Asian headdress— the kind worn by priests and dancers at Chinese New Year processions.

Terri had been given a leather bag for their picnic. She took some mangoes and papayas out of it. She carefully unwrapped a wide leaf and removed a chunk of roasted tapir, or forest pig, and lunch was served.

Yanni became more relaxed outside the view of the strange tribal people. Terri had adult social skills to navigate tribal peoples' odd looks and whispered comments to each other, but they just scared Yanni. He was seven years old after all.

"They look at me like they want to eat me," Yanni said.

Terri shivered a little at that. She rethought her policy of strict honesty with children. The vicious imagery and depictions on many of the huge stone monuments sparked her darkest imaginings. She didn't want to put them into words. These people weren't above sacrificing visiting gods just to show how much they loved them. "Me too," she said lightly, "Let's avoid anyone coming toward us with a fork and spoon."

Yanni laughed. It was the first time she had found a way to tickle him in weeks. Food, sunlight, and the flower-strewn jungle worked their natural charm, and they skipped and danced back to the ceremonial center.

Cho-lub found them somewhere near the courtyard. He seemed tense, like he needed to talk. Terri followed his pidgin and sign language as well as she could for two hours, translating for Yanni. The main chief, Satnomel, was declaring his supremacy and he wanted all the clans to declare their alliances with him. He would observe his obligations by providing much food for a feast, but all the clans had to bring their own tribute obligations as well. As a further requirement, the clans had to demonstrate their social and ceremonial status. Cho-lub wanted to present the Goddess of the Moon, Terri, as part of his clan's contribution. Terri felt the tightening anxiety as he said this.

He took them to a series of apartments near the step pyramid at the far end of the ceremonial complex, the royal precincts of the paramount lineage. The open areas of the royal neighborhood held bundles of goods and food brought in for the feast. A few lineage warriors stood guard over the wealth items, amounting to several tons of foodstuffs and finished arts and crafts goods.

He walked up the stone steps of the chief's house. A single guard waved him through, along with Terri and Yanni. Cho-lub made obeisance to the people inside the apartment. Terri and Yanni bowed respectfully. Terri always hated hierarchy but played along. The chief sat in a wooden chair. His name was Satnomel, and he did not stand to greet them. Family members and servants went about their business. Lounging near Satnomel was a person dissimilar from anyone in this tribal world, much like Terri and Yanni. Garbed in Egyptian clothing, the heavyset man wore a snail-shaped crown of fabric. He remained unsmiling and did not respond to respectful greetings.

Satnomel gave Terri and Yanni plenty of attention, looking them both up and down, his eyes glittering. Terri would know that look anywhere. Satnomel frowned when he saw the red and orange belt around Terri's waist, well aware of the ownership it implied. Terri tried not to stare back, for Satnomel had a split upper lip like a cleft palette, or hare-lip, but it may have been a mutilation to create a clan emblem in his flesh. A jade labret closed the split. Some of the monuments of the ceremonial center had pouty split lips carved in stone with labret closures, and she thought of the other men she had seen in the courtyard with this kind of labret position. This suggested to Terri that a powerful ancestor and leader of Satnomel's lineage had exhibited a natural cleft palette. Descendants emulated the divine mark artificially to denote kinship with him.

Satnomel and Cho-lub engaged in a rapid conversation of which Terri could understand very little. Yanni leaned into Terri for protection. It was clear only that Satnomel and Cho-lub were discussing the night's feasting. The strange visitor ignored all the proceedings. Eventually, Cho-lub had received all his instructions, and he bowed and left with Terri and Yanni.

Cho-lub felt the need to put all the far-flung members of his clan in action. His father was aged, the official chief of the lineage, now only involved with ceremonial events. Leadership fell on Cho-lub and his brothers and cousins, many of whom lived in distant villages. Cho-lub's anxiety was palpable, which did nothing to lower Terri's anxiety. Her dreams had been silent on her progress through this timeline; she had not dreamed of Laney Joe. But her waking, intuitive consciousness told her that this place was building up to some kind of a crunch point. Something big was going to happen.

Terri asked about the mysterious, Egyptian-garbed companion of Satnomel. When he understood what Terri was asking, Cho-lub took a deep breath and gave Terri and Yanni the short version. The Egyptian was a powerful ally of Satnomel. Satnomel and all his ancestors were powerful shamans. The leaders of all clans who are shamans gain more spiritual and political power in the inevitable contest for power among the clans. Satnomel with his jaguar spirit familiar had traveled the world above, the trance world, until he had found a very strong ally and brought him back. That was why the mysterious person was here. And it was clear that the goal of the visitor was to ensure Satnomel's assumption of power.

They arrived at the stone room on the edge of the courtyard. There Cho-lub explained their roles in the ceremonial. Terri would present herself as the Goddess of the Moon to the people assembled at the pyramid. Cho-lub used many expansive, wide gestures to make his points. She still understood very few of his spoken words, and she concentrated heavily on his gestures. Such a demonstration by her at the ceremony would secure the clan's prestige for a generation. Terri would live in luxury as a symbol of the clan and of the moon for the rest of her life. Terri grew suspicious of his lack of gestures or references to Yanni.

What about Yanni? She pointed and gestured to Yanni. She claimed him as her child and her inseparable companion, a magic being in his own right. Cho-lub debated that with many negations. Any child was a wonderful thing, of course, but ultimately they were subservient to the lives and goals of their adults. Surely Terri knew and believed that? She squinted at Cho-lub with great skepticism. He went on, it was always the way of Cho-lub and his people. Cho-lub repeated his gestures until their meaning was clear. The young chief held his arms in a cradling position and slowly raised them high while lifting his head and eyes upward as though gazing at the moon.

Words weren't necessary at that point. Yanni the child god would ascend to the goddess in the night sky in gratitude from the worshippers on Earth. Anybody in any culture would know that Cho-lub's gestures meant that Yanni was going to be sacrificed.

Terri felt herself fainting while reaching behind herself for Yanni. He darted toward the door before she could touch him, but he was met just outside by a few lineage warriors who grabbed him and carried him away. Terri thought her last glimpse of Yanni was her last tie to anything familiar in life. She could feel the onrush of disorientation, as she settled into the floor as into the grave. She'd never felt much anger in life, her emotions running to frustration dissolving into resignation. But now, at the very nadir, the bottom, of life she found a core of anger. She knew she'd need a lot of it to save herself and Yanni. She'd already made a few scant preparations for escape, a bug-out plan, and she must not let them go, pathetic as they might be.

Cho-lub looked regretful. Terri breathed shallowly, and her vision narrowed to sharp points. When she recovered rational thought, she could only beg for Yanni's life, taking deeper breaths to build her energy.

Cho-lub insisted she prove her divinity to guarantee the success of his clan. Terri indicated that they should kill her, too, if they sacrificed Yanni. What did she care about his stupid clan? Then she found the presence of mind to bargain with him for Yanni's life. Rising to stand on the stone floor, she used very clear gestures to indicate to Cho-lub that if they found another sacrifice she'd prove her divinity—though she had no idea how she'd accomplish that—and live among the clan as he wished, but only with Yanni, not without him. Cho-lub refused at first, but he did look confused and uncertain. Perhaps he still thought he held all the cards in this game of life and death. Probably he had only dealt with women out of his lusts.

Terri loosened her loincloth, bent over to lower it, and stepped out of it. Weeping but resolute, she stepped over to Cho-lub, raised her eyes, and captured his gaze. She raised one slender ballet leg to the side, wrapped it around his hips, and captured his loins.

21

Faringway and Roller reviewed their predicament while Ah-noot floated them and Kheeg-ah-tah around the countryside. Kheeg-ah-tah's camp far below stayed in view as a kind of anchor, ringed in incense-smoke that did not dissipate. It remained as a secure and concealing base for them and exit point from the trance world. Ah-noot and Kheeg-ah-tah chatted about the herbs and medicinal plants they encountered and peeked in on the breeding grounds of the birds and small creatures in the marshes and creeks. They giggled and pointed out the chicks in their nests and the squirmy tadpoles in the water. Both master herbalists, they traded tips and secrets as they played.

"I still can't comprehend this space we traverse cognitively," Roller said.

"I'm farther behind than you, Roller," Faringway said, "but I'm sure we are here physically as well as mentally, at least in part."

"*Tck...tck,*" said Roller telepathically.

"Your quirks are good reality testing, Roller," Faringway said with a laugh. Roller looked puzzled.

"Just trying to figure it out, Faringway."

"May I help, even a little?" Faringway looked intently at Roller, "I've been doing some thinking in the few weeks since Kheeg-ah-tah dragged me into the trance world, and some of it indeed scans."

"*Tck...tck.*"

"That's better. I did a little research into the paranormal before embarking on my moneymaking scheme spotlighting ghosts with Terri and Laney Joe. Don't you see? These tribal shamans from way back have unlocked the DNA closet of psychic powers in all human beings, stuff Western science is only now beginning to address."

"You're sounding like me not so long ago."

Faringway gave him the trance world glare. "Except I am not speculating like you were. I have facts." His forefinger went straight up to counter any response from Roller. He went on, "Western civilization took halting steps toward the paranormal with the Rhine experiments at Duke University in the nineteen-freakin'-twenties. The Rhines were a husband and wife team of psychological researchers."

"Right," agreed Roller. "They were the card flippers. They had subjects guess the card patterns of cards before they turned them up. They coined the term extrasensory perception...ESP."

"You got it. They gained positive results published obscurely in a career's worth of dull scholarly papers—something I've warned you about, eh?"

"Yes." Roller smiled. "Statistical significance at the 0.05 alpha level, beta testing—nobody understands that. Single-blind, double-blind, unconscious cueing... It's the very pedantry and lameness of the scientific method that kept Las Vegas from assassinating them."

Faringway guffawed. "Sometimes ignorance can be a protective thing. But back to the Rhines—after all the academic debates and hurly-burly, they retired. But a coterie of committed followers thought that the Rhines had opened a door to new worlds, and they continued research into all forms of the paranormal at places like Stanford University and the American Society for Psychical Research."

"Ah, yes," Roller said, "the bright grad students who do the backing and filling for the dotty professors."

"Everything can be reduced to a movie script with you," Faringway snapped, "but it so happens that the CIA didn't discover them until the 1980s. And when they did, oh brother, it was a super-secret group, and no more published papers. The CIA wanted broad-ranging research to look into rooms and locales and see what was going on—enemies, friends, you name it. They let the researchers investigate ancient seers to gain clues as to how they spied out the past, present, and future in the process called clairvoyance. They were impressed with the Oracle of Delphi, but they hit pay dirt with Nostradamus, the famous seer of the 1500s who predicted the rise of both Napoleon and Hitler. He described how he entered trance and laid out his method in his papers. They weren't revealed until after his death in order to avoid accusations of witchcraft. In essence, his method was simple. He stilled his mind, then stared into a bowl of water mounted on a brass tripod. A lit candle stood nearby."

"There are other ways," Roller said, thinking of the indigo-footed mussels.

"Fine. The point is that knowing the procedure meant anyone could enter the state—induced psychic powers, if you will, versus natural-born psychic powers. Anyone could become clairvoyant. The CIA liked it so much, they dubbed it remote viewing, RV; and, in the manner of all other militaristic institutions, they declared the program a failure, classified everything, and ended the program. No telling what they are doing with it now."

"And that's it?" Roller asked, wanting to hear more. His curiosity always made him bolder, a buffer against anyone noticing his fear.

"Of course not," said Faringway, smiling and enjoying a delicious irony. "The unemployed civilian researchers formed a commercial business to make bucks off their top-secret knowledge. Ha!"

"Oh, like police psychics helping law enforcement find kidnapped kids and murder victims?" said Roller.

"There was some of that mundane stuff, true," said Faringway, "But there was also some stuff that resists explanation to this day."

"Like what?"

"Here's the part that sticks in my memory cells. After the breakup of the Soviet Union, the Russians approached the civilian business concern with a contract to help them find a lost space vehicle. The US had a similar incident, but never bothered to investigate it with the remote viewing crowd. The Russians thought the incidents were similar, so the remote viewers looked at both of them. In March of 1989, the unmanned Soviet space probe *Phobos II* was lost to all contact as it entered orbit around the planet Mars. In identical fashion, the US Mars *Observer* craft was lost upon entering Mars orbit on August 20, 1993."

"A team of remote viewers attempted contact with *Phobos II* as the Russians had hired them to do. The team viewed the space craft successfully, and witnessed two objects approaching the space probe—one from the surface of Mars and one orbiting in Mars space. The second object projected a beam at the craft which damaged it internally, eventually leading to its destruction. Ditto the American spacecraft, although I think with that one, only a single alien object approached the space probe."

Faringway shook his head thoughtfully. "No matter what you think of alien life, the remote viewers saw these incidents from years earlier as though they were happening in real time. Did they see through time or did they make up stories while in hypnotic trance? Either way, the Russians liked their stories well enough to pay their fees."

"Impressive," Roller said, "but what's that got to do with Neolithic Siberia?"

"Don't you see? The spectacular results validate the learning. The remote viewers learned how to induce psychic powers in humans from researching Nostradamus and others, but the shamans of prehistory either unlocked them natively or learned how to induce them by learning from ancestors…" Here, Faringway seemed to grope for words, "And somehow, they condensed that generational knowledge like locked files. And all their chanting, molecules, mystical tripods, and pools of water are algorithms for the same thing—opening the gate to that world beyond all ken. Psychic powers are latent in all humans by virtue of DNA and manifest in a few."

Roller saw Faringway's look of total absorption. Roller had seen that faraway look in his eyes before when Faringway had been working on a difficult programming problem. He had been in the programmer version of "The Zone."

Faringway came out of it quickly. "Either way—induced or inherited—it means human beings have latent or manifest wild psychic powers. Welcome to your new world, Roller."

"Most of it is dry academic knowledge, really. What we need is a practical way to find our lost team members and transport them with us to our home timeline," Roller said.

Faringway smiled.

22

The Western Desert had outcrops of rock, mostly of sandstone, that projected above the dunes six to ten feet, sometimes twenty feet. The outcrops formed ridges that ran along for a few hundred feet but were never substantial enough to form a hill or mesa. Windblown sand chipped and pecked away at the sandstone and added to the oceanic mass of loose sand in the desert. At times, the dunes overwhelmed the rock features, burying them for an age, then blowing away again to expose them for another age. Laney Joe huddled in the lee of one such stone projection, a dry rib of the world. Behind him, the dune fields stretched to a darkening horizon.

Laney Joe fled the temple of On to avoid the beast Horemheb, as had many of the other priests just before Horemheb sent soldiers to attack. Thann-us was found dead in a small camp near the Third Cataract—not hacked to death by swords, just dead. That zone was so far from the delta that it should have been safe from a pursuer. It led

Laney Joe to believe that Horemheb had tracked them down in the trance state, not with trackers and good intuition. But if so, why did Horemheb not have a talisman of the victim he was trying to observe? Lor-naat had required such to observe Akhenaton, and that is why Laney Joe and the others had traveled to the royal court of Amarna and had gained the golden pectoral. The master and evil magician, Horemheb, had powers beyond those possessed by Lor-naat. But to what extent? Laney Joe did not know now, and when would he ever know? The thought gave him a shiver of terror every time. How could he know his deadly enemy to the fullest degree? He had to increase his skills in the trance world to improve his defense.

The wind calmed, and the desert cooled. There shone no moon but many stars. At last, Laney Joe sat unafraid, seeming to settle under the cloak of darkness. Indeed, Horemheb would not need to approach at night. But the jackals and the wolves might offer themselves as Laney Joe's helpers. He found comfort in the rocks, the sand, and the night. He rested comfortably in the dark and with the fire, now burnt to embers. A few shooting stars scratched sparks against the vault of night. How could a man feel so alive on the darkest night?

He had removed Lor-naat's brass tripod, bowl, and a supply of candles from the temple room. Laney Joe was barely capable of entering trance on his own. And there had been so much more for Lor-naat to teach him. He set out the apparatus before him near the fading fire. He got up to pour a small amount of precious water from one of the ceramic water vessels he had brought with him. The vessels were packed in leather bags with straps, wrapped in fabric to buffer them from breakage, and that kept the water cool. The water was the heaviest item in his kit but necessary for pedestrian travel in the desert.

He lit a candle from the embers and affixed it firmly in the sand near the tripod and water bowl. His hand fell on the golden pectoral that had cost Lor-naat and others their lives. It was of no use in his trance making now, and he thought since Horemheb didn't know of it, nor had ever touched it, it could not be used by Horemheb to trace him. But then again, Horemheb had other means of doing just that, and the unsettling feelings returned to Laney Joe.

He chanted and chanted, staring at the surface of the water made golden by the nearby candle and ember light. *Release a thought, release a thought, sink deeper.*

The events of Marfa and those he had seen in the trance world had a few similarities. Could it be that the power of the Marfa storm and the capacities of trance were features of the same dimension and refractions of the same ball of universal glue? Was trance the universal force bridging from gluons and muons to pulsars and black holes? Did it give texture to space? And above all, could sentients move through that field with agency? Surely, Horemheb could travel through the trance space as well as the ancient shamans and seers, but could Horemheb be brought to justice? Was Laney Joe feeling a call to justice—something he'd never received himself—or was this a drive toward bitter revenge? Could Laney Joe bring justice to Horemheb?

A far-off jackal yipped once. *Was that yes or no?* The wind whispered, enough to disturb the candle flame protected on the lee side of the rock formation. Laney Joe reached to cup the flame and shield it from the wind as the embers brightened briefly, its lungs taking a warm, bright breath. The wind whispered, and whispered, and whispered....

Laney Joe felt himself floating away from a comfortable, secure home and saw the lee-side encampment below. The landscape became vague lumps of rock and piles of sand. Falcons swooped above it with him, along with a few retreating owls. He had entered the trance world, and the sensation was of flying. The atmosphere and the landscape below became clearer as he drove farther into the dreamlike state of trance. He began to believe he had agency in another dimension of reality. The birds flew all around him. The day shift of aerial predators was taking over from the night shift, although it was still night. The falcons seemed to be inviting him to join them. A falcon flew up to him, bated, and stared intently at him. The falcon, large and magnificent, had huge brown eyes which matched the feathers on his wing covers and back. His cheeks were white with a deep-black band of short feathers arching from the back of his beak around his eyes and bordering his neck to end in tips pointing forward. The shape of the black bands looked like hieroglyphics, which was probably where the Egyptians got them for their writing. His talons were curved like blue-gray steel, now tucked respectfully against his belly while flying. His tail and lower back showed lateral bands of black, brown, and white, all above a light gray belly pied with black spots. The lordly creature whirled and drew Laney Joe along with him at a high rate of speed. They had the comfort level of old friends.

The falcon and Laney Joe proceeded to the royal court of Amarna, Akhenaton's former capital. The palace was quiet and almost empty. Why had the falcon brought him here? He was revisiting the site where he had first viewed a scene from trance. Perhaps it was the tug of the golden pectoral he had received here. Laney Joe saw a stripling pharaoh, the successor to Akhenaton, moving out of the palace to return the capital to Thebes. The time of this viewing was not long after Horemheb had assassinated Akhenaton, and succession had proceeded as normal. Why hadn't Horemheb taken over the throne immediately? It was clear that Horemheb sought political power, but politics was not the only source for the power he already had. Why did he seek more? Laney Joe began to think that Horemheb, a powerful warlock, did not really belong in Egypt. He did not fit.

The falcon continued driving their flight eastward, toward the dawn and sunrise, beyond Deir el-Medina, another site familiar to Laney Joe. They swooped low, and there he saw the body of his marvelous friend Khan-ep in the sand. His skin was wrinkled and leathery, beginning to mummify under the desert sun. He had been the noble priest who had sought him out, who had shared this land of Egypt with him, and who had started him on this glorious and frightful journey.

Fear, anger, uncertainty, emptiness, and sorrow gusted through Laney Joe, hollowing him. He witnessed a flood of images as though the Earth unleashed all its moments in time, all its experiences, from a vault deep within its core. The falcon looked at him, blinked, and kept flying. The other birds had left them by now, and the empowering, beautiful, and thrilling sensations were of a dream of flying.

His trance journey suddenly became a kaleidoscope of all time—fractured, flying away, recombining in sequences of history, and increasing in volume and intensity. The falcon led him into it confidently. He was the full-partner trance traveler the falcon needed. The experience and its sensations comprised an event beyond Marfa, like a lucid dream gone out of control in which the dreamer wakes gasping for breath. He expected momentarily to awaken beside Terri. His falcon whirled around him flapping its wings, staring intently into his face. In that moment of psychic lucidity, Laney Joe knew with certainty that this was the Horus falcon, flown out of myth as the guardian of Osiris, the mummified but living god, and now the guardian of this swirling place. He was now and forever his animal familiar.

The Horus falcon took him on a great parabolic arc. Like two ballistic missiles, they seemed to fly away from Earth but then arched down toward a great hole or tunnel in the Earth. Hexagon-shaped panels of some unknown material lined the mouth of the tunnel. The Horus falcon flew with urgency, diving with air screaming through his feathers as though homing in on a pigeon. They flew at full-speed freefall, headlong into darkness. They gradually leveled out, zooming into a cavern or some immense space at once closed but vast. The bottom, or floor, of the cavern seemed to move or flow like some oceanic underground river. Instead of water, Laney Joe saw particles with colors and imagery that occasionally sparkled or shone. There were also larger panels with imagery moving and flowing over their surfaces, records of events in time—perhaps every event in every time. Laney Joe knew then that he and the Horus falcon had flown into the fabled Hall of Records of which Khan-ep had spoken. The Horus falcon shrieked, and Laney Joe knew from intuition that the Horus falcon was its guardian.

Horemheb and Laney Joe saw each other at the same time. Horemheb stood on a promontory of ice or glass above the writhing streams of time forming the glacial river. A child-sized humanoid creature stood with Horemheb, pointing up at them. The streams extended outward to the vaulted walls and ceiling. Hexagon panel pillars rose into darkness. Horemheb directed and controlled the streams of time and imagery by uttering incantations and gesturing. He seemed to be downloading them directly into his mind.

Laney Joe interrupted Horemheb by focusing his hatred at him. Horemheb gave an animal roar, pulled an arm away from a gesture he was holding, and seemed to deflect something hurled at him—Laney Joe's anger. The air in the cavern became much warmer. Laney Joe knew he must avoid having Horemheb's little black object pointed at him. He orbited Horemheb erratically at a high rate of speed. The Horus falcon gave its high, screeching call; it had identified its prey, the violator of Earth's knowledge.

The time rivers sped forward in blurring motion—none of them under control— perhaps trying to escape Horemheb's control over them. Horemheb fumbled in a pocket of his robe while the Horus falcon dove on Horemheb with its talons grown into bronze scimitars, trailing flames. Horemheb fended the falcon off with energy he seemed to project from his eyes, while still fumbling for his small black object, the murder weapon used on Akhenaton and many others. The falcon made sharp flying maneuvers, picking up speed and diving at Horemheb and the small humanoid creature beside him from different attack angles. Part of one of Horemheb's energy bolts hit Laney Joe, sending him tumbling in space, his face burning as if on fire. He felt a great drain of energy and a grain of fear. He pushed it away forcefully, driving back into his concentration, his mind racing with the moment.

Horemheb opened a hidden portal that was reflective like a full-length closet mirror. The falcon swooped on the small humanoid figure, and it bumped its head on the side of the portal trying to run through it. Horemheb swung a fist at the Horus falcon at close quarters. It was an ineffective gesture and didn't have enough time to bring the small murder ray to bear. In an instant, the Horus falcon sliced the small creature to shreds like meat through a meat grinder. The creature shrieked once—Laney Joe seemed to hear it in his mind—before falling to pieces. The portal aperture closed behind Horemheb. Horemheb had scarcely defended his defenseless companion. *Add coward to Horemheb's list of malign traits,* Laney Joe thought.

The Horus falcon screamed back to Laney Joe in victory and drove its beak into his shoulder. The leaping splash of blood and electric flash of pain pulled him at eye-blurring speed across hundreds or thousands of miles of the trance world to his stone ridge encampment and out of trance.

The encampment had been overturned in a violent sandstorm in the night. The tripod and bowl had been blown into crevices in the rock, and the water bag, initially wedged into a niche in the rock, was half buried by sand. The golden pectoral, which Laney Joe kept on his person, was secure. The candle and the ashes from the fire were gone. Laney Joe gathered the few items remaining and left the rocks for an oasis and, possibly, treatment for his wound. The distant, high cry of a falcon bade him goodbye.

23

Horemheb fought his way out of the transfer chamber on Thonlus breathing hard. He concentrated on an image of the Meno family hold while making connection with his mother. He found her, and she was awake.

"Kenli was killed on Earth!" he cried. "Listen, their forces are powerful, and they hold them in secret until they can pull them out and destroy an innocent spirit familiar. I found the Atlanteans' Hall of Records, but it was guarded by strong forces. Of course, no non-shaman will ever find it; the portal locks are in the trance space. The hall is where they killed Kenli, right when I was getting started. The trail left by the Atlanteans was right there before me! I won't be as unprepared or patient next time."

Lun said nothing. Horemheb detected her typical callousness.

"Oh, no. I'm not bouncing off your stone walls again," Horemheb said, cautioning her not to play games with him.

Lun was amused. "What? I gave you free rein to do anything on the mission, and you merely fumbled away Kenli? To the vats with you," she laughed.

"Strategic planning doesn't come easily when I'm threatened constantly with being thrown into the vats! You give me vague advice, 'find a powerful shaman,' and that's been nothing but a diversion. The shamans I have found are among those few aberrant ones who are seeking political power. They are too much like us."

Lun met him in the foyer and they strolled into the rear chambers, talking. Lun's serenity was imperturbable. Horemheb knew that was a weapon. Her enemies couldn't get to her mind in any way that would disturb her or distort her thinking. It was a quality that infuriated Horemheb, largely because he did not inherit it.

"In my opinion, you are forgetting your training," Lun stated sweetly. "When was the last time you practiced expansive meditation? You don't know how to make friends with the local shamans. They can help you because they know the turf and would answer your questions if you simply asked."

Horemheb shrugged.

"Lacking help with the local wise ones, your best detector is your own meditation—the kind that can observe the entire planet," she continued. "Take some time and let the awareness tendrils encircle the planet. See what you pick up. You will gain a serviceable psychic map of the planet that way, too."

"Perhaps. I'll try anything," he returned. "I adjusted some of the monuments the local shamans use for navigation, so I'll have to revisit all of them to get my own map straight first. But what I want most is to show the Aat a strong, artistic Egyptian empire that fulfills the promise of a rich planet, even if the Atlanteans did most of the work setting it up ages ago. There's nothing else there that serves my purpose. The planet can still fall into the lap of the Meno. Back me in that strategy, please, and watch me win."

"Your strategy is merely your hobby, but your goal is loyal and worthy," Lun sighed. "And the Aat are inscrutable. You'll probably need the help, or at least the silence, of the earthly shamans. You decide. And go with the expansive meditation. Trance is our best weapon."

Horemheb was already walking away from her, believing that he had won a concession from Lun, or at least her silence.

Laney Joe sat under a bush in the desert. By subtraction, the shade of the bush was the perfect extravagant gift of the sun. It covered no more than the area of his body while he sat. His wound was healing rapidly with very little pain. Far above, the Horus falcon wheeled and screeched joyously, seeming very happy to have discovered Laney Joe. Afternoon cumulus clouds dotted the sky—the only blemishes on the brilliant blue dome.

Laney Joe was near Deir el-Medina. He had returned there to work the stone of the new tombs with his stoneworker friends, or at least a group that would tolerate him, although he more than paid his way with his hard work. The villagers also liked his pet falcon. Laney Joe explored the Zen-like meditation of chipping stone endlessly. The earthly material was shaped for spiritual purposes.

Today, he sat only with the determination to rise into the fullness of the gift he had been given. Even that was a process of letting go. He felt now that the gift had been given not by a set of mystic priests whose paths on Earth had been followed to their ends, but by the wider universe, removing distractions from him until this core reality remained. This was his fate—this Egypt, this time, this home. And what was this home? It was the shade of a bush in the desert. His gratitude knew no bounds. Until now, he had had no direction in life, no purpose, and few kind words of encouragement from anyone. He had seen many faces of hate. The cosmic lesson seemed to have been to keep a healthy distance from human beings. But then there was Terri. She had so embraced him, seeking to learn his secrets as he did hers. Perhaps they were fools colliding, but so be it; he didn't care. And then she had been taken from him by some snakelike coil in space and time beyond his comprehension. All desire had been stripped forcibly from him.

Still, here he sat, the very soul of contentment. He had nothing else but this shade, and the larger realm. He touched the golden pectoral. He saw the shadows of the tiny leaves shaking, their pointed ends blurring when they trembled in the slight breeze. *Trembling and blurring... trembling and blurring...*

The Horus falcon greeted him in trance, circling as he rose and rose directly above the shady bush. Laney Joe's awareness seemed to expand 360 degrees around him, and he felt like he saw all the molecules of air as they swept by. The desert, mountains, and oceans were all spread over the soft bed of the Earth. The view expanded and expanded, until the view turned back on itself and encompassed Laney Joe in the center of a sphere. He felt nodes of energy in the movement of people clustering in cities, herbivore herds that combed the surface of the land, and whales migrating in huge pods through every ocean. Channels and giant tubes seemed to tie the Earth together and tunnel through it. Other avenues entered the network from beyond. Light and buzzing electrical energy flashed everywhere. Glimpses of other times came to him. He saw an Earth with cities powered entirely by Tesla coils and another with shining solar energy. Another time channel showed Earth entering a new mountain building phase, or orogeny, and hundreds of volcanoes emitted clouds of ash and gas pitching it into nuclear winter and darkness.

The Horus falcon screeched for his attention, mercifully not drawing blood this time. Laney Joe came back, a trifle unwillingly, to the merciful bush. In front of it lay two desert doves, freshly taken by the falcon. The falcon landed, picked up one bird, and moved it a respectful distance away for his feeding. Laney Joe got up to look for firewood, carefully avoiding taking any of the branches of the bush.

24

Terri dreamed that a pyre flared on the base of an overturned buttercup. But the buttercup was one-hundred feet high. The pyre roared higher, and flaming rocks launched from the fire. The mound grew to a volcano. Flying serpents with the heads of snarling jaguars zoomed above the ceremonial courtyard, and bound captives screamed and fell on the table of the step pyramid. Huge stone heads pushed out of the ground, becoming giants forty feet high, wielding clubs and pounding the earth to make giant booms that echoed off the distant mountains. Long-haired warriors with spears rushed by, rank after rank, looking for violence. The Great Egyptian floated above the scene, lightning bolts flashing from both outstretched hands. Terri looked everywhere for Yanni but couldn't see him anywhere.

She awoke in desperation. She pushed Cho-lub off her, pointed with one finger out the door and shouted, "Yanni!"

Cho-lub grabbed his garments and ran out the door like a misbehaving teenager fleeing punishment. Terri stood and stumbled to the water pot for a drink. She looked at her wadded-up loincloth on the stone floor. The things couldn't protect one's modesty if they tried. She kicked it aside contemptuously and ran out the door. She had a rush of feeling that she possessed more power nude than bound by a loincloth. Her dreams, including this one, made her feel naked before great powers. Perhaps the lesson was that she only had herself without armor of any kind to challenge the power of the universe. Feeling naked simply reminded her of the vulnerability everyone felt most of the time. She raised her head and walked across the courtyard.

The entire ceremonial complex was lit by torches and cooking fires. Indeed, a bonfire burned on the high mound, its light reflecting off the bottoms of the low overcast clouds above. Drums pounded their rhythms, but the stone heads remained in place for now. Crowds of people from all lineages came in groups, most bearing baskets of offerings to their gods and the great chief Satnomel. Warriors of the various lineages assembled in ranks or informal groups. They commonly held lances tipped with sharp, flaked obsidian heads. They also bore large wooden clubs with bashing heads set with blades of razor-sharp obsidian set into the wood. Warriors and officials wore flamboyant headdresses of many macaw feathers, bright fabrics, and shining gemstones.

Terri knew where she was expected, so she made her way toward the step pyramid at the end of the complex.

"Terri, Terri!" Yanni came running toward her, still trailing the ropes with which they had tied him. "Cho-lub had the guards free me! I guess he changed his mind."

"I helped him change his mind, I fought for you. But you stood up for yourself, young man, and you won." Terri hugged him with tears flowing and her body a quivering mass of naked sweat. She couldn't bring herself to explain everything to Yanni in detail.

She dropped to her knees and looked him straight in the eye. "Now listen to the plan, and do exactly as I say, Yanni. Run out to our picnic monument out above the river. Don't let anyone stop you. I left the leather picnic bag in the little cave behind the statue. It has our space clothes in it and a little fruit for our escape. Put your clothes on and wait for me there or nearby. If anyone but me comes looking, hide. If I never come, escape on one of the trader canoes. Your superpower right now is hiding. Run."

Yanni's eyes grew wider and wider. "Wow," he said and took off.

Terri couldn't flee with him because she drew too much attention. With Yanni safer, she could pay off Cho-lub somehow and make her own escape.

The festival presentation was on the wide step, or table, of the pyramid, about a third of the way to the top of the structure. The actual top of the stone mass held a bonfire attended by slaves with fuel logs. The fire was sufficient to mirror the one on the high mound at the opposite end of the ceremonial precinct. Lineage members from all the districts of the clans gathered at the base of the pyramid, which was well-lit by torches. Large cooking fires burned at various points around the courtyard.

Cho-lub found her at the base of the pyramid, and they mounted the steps to the presentation stage. Several of the clans and groups chanted as they carried bundled gifts to the presentation platform. Only the highest-ranking members of the clans were allowed on the pyramid. But only the warriors of Satnomel's lineage were allowed on the steps of the pyramid.

Satnomel and the Egyptian stood near the top of the walking steps. On either side of the steps, as they opened out on the flat platform, two nervous adult jaguars crouched, restrained by ropes, whipping their tails and glaring at everyone who walked past. The jaguar undoubtedly was the totemic animal of Satnomel's chiefly clan and also Satnomel's spirit familiar. To Terri, Satnomel seemed to have designs on her, but she couldn't think about that now. Her nudity made her a little too vulnerable for the formal occasion and Satnomel's gaze. She walked to her position behind the lineage group with her arms crossed over her stomach and her head down. Satnomel wore an overshirt with eagle feathers tied onto it at intervals. The Egyptian was impassive. Arriving lineage heads filed along the table toward the corner. Cho-lub's lineage, with his father and senior relations, formed the group nearest the center and the walking steps. Cho-lub gestured for Terri to stand behind the lineage group until he was ready for her to step out. Cho-lub's lineage had done everything to demonstrate heightened wealth and prestige, and it was cementing its relationship with Satnomel's lineage—hence Terri, the goddess of the Moon and minion of Cho-lub's powerful clan.

Satnomel gestured to start the festival. The drumming stopped. Warriors brought two bound female teenage slaves up to the platform. They screamed and writhed in their bindings. The warriors backed out of the way. The Egyptian pointed a small black object at the sacrifices and the slaves screamed, quivered as though shocked, and dropped lifeless to the platform. One of the bodies slipped over the edge of the flat table and rolled most of the way to the bottom. The crowd roared as other slaves retrieved their bodies and carried them to the festival fires. They would become part of the ceremonial feast of this cannibal chiefdom.

Terri saw the murders, turned, and retched. They were the substitutes for Yanni. She would never overcome the guilt. At least Yanni would not have to know this. She staggered, about to faint, but out of the corner of her eye saw that Cho-lub had seen her reaction. He gestured violently toward the front, angry. She knew what she had to do. She wanted to die, but instead she took deep breaths. She walked slowly, head down, to the front of the platform at the head of the flight of stairs, between the two jaguars.

Terri didn't know if she was deep within herself or far outside herself looking in. Her life might end abruptly if that evil Egyptian swung his black object around toward her. *Now demonstrate something,* she told herself. Divinity? What was that? She could only do what her body knew to do without question. Her reflexes were trained, and her muscles, ligaments, and joints cultivated to perform in the only way she knew. She rose *en pointe*, and pain fired through her feet as she seemed to grow to about six feet in height instantly. The crowd gasped, seeing clearly the double horns of the Moon goddess in her toes.

Ignoring the pain, and everything peripheral, Terri began her finest showcase solo from the apex of her dance career. It was the solo she had performed perhaps a hundred times. She couldn't forget it. If her mind forgot it, her feet, legs, and arms would perform it unerringly for her. The crowd saw a dance that could not exist; they had no cultural preparation for it. They saw Terri in a coating of perspiration that gave a high gloss to her nudity, and her limbs extended beyond human limits. They were electrified—definitely outside themselves—in the realm of the divine. They witnessed how the goddess danced in her heaven beyond the moon as it was now revealed to them.

Terri knew that ballet had been created in the castles and mansions of the nobility of Europe. Every aspect of training and choreography was intended to make movements and bodies appear otherworldly and unnatural. The deeper goal was to prove that the nobility, who created these creatures, were themselves more than human and above ordinary human beings. Superhumans. Now, in another timeline, or perhaps in another world, Terri saw how that philosophy was almost literally true.

She made *grand jeté*, flying leaps, to either side, and the jaguars cowered away from her. She ran *en pointe* back to stage center as she had many times with electric pain shooting in her toes, but it was a very familiar pain. She had made the movement so many times, though never with her life on the line. She made prancing toe-walks *en pointe,* and in agony, to stage front and upstage. She departed from ballet briefly to borrow from modern technique in making cartwheels left and to right. A thin line of blood was thrown onto the stone stage in each direction from her feet. She tried the pirouettes called for by the choreography, but without toe shoes, her bleeding toes merely twisted on the rough stone and would not serve as a pivot. She almost lost her balance but recovered instantly without being noticed. She substituted simple gestures to bridge their place in the choreography.

She ended the dance in a humble crouch, her wrists and hands settling gently to the stone table like flower petals falling gently into a pool of water, until they lay relaxed and crossed on the stone platform. She managed to end smoothly, without twitching from the pain coursing through her body like lightning. Bizarrely, the two jaguars roared as one. Then the crowd took it up, roaring in exultation. Satnomel walked forward with his arms raised. His fingers were crooked jaggedly in cat-claw hands like jaguars leaping on prey with their claws extended. He received the adulation of the crowd, taking full credit for the divine dance. Terri remained crouching humbly on the stage.

The Egyptian stepped forward, too, but he turned and pointed the small black object at the assembled lineage chiefs and leading families on the platform. They added to the roaring of the crowd with their death screams and their arms and legs shaking and falling in spasms to the platform. Cho-lub was among them. The Egyptian fired again and again to kill them all. A few noblemen fell over the edge and rolled limply down the stone slope to the base of the pyramid. By now, the crowds in the courtyard had fallen silent in shock. Satnomel's power maneuver was complete, or so he thought. Satnomel, in league with the Egyptian, had killed all the lineage heads in a public display of power that allowed him to take over all the clans and rule them. The other clans had never trusted him, but they thought nothing of assembling en masse in their capital. They had also never imagined the Egyptian's small black murder weapon.

The crowd was silent in complete disbelief. When the roaring of the jaguars brought them back, people ran back and forth in fear and anger. Two spears arched through the night and hit the platform, their obsidian tips shattering on the stone. Satnomel waved his arms to bring order to the crowd as he walked back and forth. The Egyptian stood back with his arms crossed. Warriors of rival factions began attacking each other. Satnomel's warriors were too few to stop the fighting.

Terri saw the violent chaos as an opportunity. Keeping a careful eye on the Egyptian, she kept low and trotted along the platform side until she got to the corner. Looking back, she saw the Egyptian sigh and vanish in the air. The sight made her stop momentarily. The pause was all Satnomel needed to catch up with her, grab her around the waist, lift her like a doll, and retreat back along the table toward the central stairway. There, a group of Satnomel's warriors formed a rank at the head of the steps and fought the opposing clan warriors moving up the slope of the pyramid. Satnomel wanted to hide behind his warriors with his prize, Terri. He was powerful, and she could not escape his grip.

He set her down and she kneed him heavily in the groin. He gave a cry and doubled over. This time, she didn't hesitate and ran along the table of the pyramid and around the corner as fast as her injured feet would allow. She was assisted by an impromptu slave revolt at the top of the pyramid where they used fuel logs to lever the burning fuel on the bonfire down the steep stairs of the structure. As the burning, smoking logs rolled down the stairway to the platform, into the air, and onto the courtyard, warriors, clan members, and slaves scattered at high speed. Terri let herself down the rough slope of the pyramid, bracing with her hands. She moved to the side, at right angles to the burning logs and fuel.

Reaching the bottom, she trotted painfully at a crouch along the side of the pyramid. She was seen by no one, as all the tribal people were occupied with the burning collapse of their society. She crossed the low stone perimeter wall of the temple complex, rose upright, and ran toward the picnic monument and Yanni.

The boy broke out of the forest cover near the monument screaming in relief when he saw her. She scooped him up and ran with him the rest of the way to the monument. He wore his modern clothes and T-shirt with the superhero face on its front.

His story poured out of him. "The leather bag was in front of the little cave—the monkeys found it and took all the fruit. The clothes were scattered, but I found them all. My shorts were on an ant hill, and I found your panties on a tree branch."

Terri felt a return of queasiness at the thought of monkeys pawing and sniffing her panties, but she pulled them on with the rest of her gear. They left quickly for the river. The adrenaline pumping within her was wearing off, and the growing pain in her feet slowed her and left her barely able to take a step. They made slow progress, carefully watching the trail behind them. The covering darkness was their best ally.

Near dawn, they slipped over the bow of a trader canoe loaded for departure. Terri's plan for the canoe was to hide on it, away from the steering gear in the stern, and reveal themselves when underway, perhaps farther from shore than the trader could reasonably decide to return and deliver them to Satnomel. They were both asleep when the canoe left dock as the sun came up.

After a few hours, they crawled out from under cargo coverings near the bow and made their way modestly toward the trader in the steersman's perch in the stern, waving in friendly fashion. The trader naturally expressed astonishment at the discovery of two very strange people waking up in his canoe on that first morning of the voyage. He had no other crew members.

But the trader named Tracco quickly enjoyed the discovery of the two stowaways when, by gesture and sign language, Terri and Yanni offered to assist in the paddling. With every stroke of the paddle, Terri gained another breath of liberation. Compared to that, callouses and backache were nothing. Her swollen toes and feet gradually returned to their somewhat bent normal positions with frequent soakings in seawater as she watched carefully for nibbling fish.

Their days on the canoe steadily improved their attitudes and health. Terri and Yanni gave up knowing where they were going or even caring about it. They stayed on the canoe when the trader beached and walked inland to trade with villagers. He traded tropical fruit for the shell jewelry manufactured by people living near the coast, woven mats, rugs and other craft items. Terri and Yanni eased off on his supplies of fruit, preferring instead the fish caught plentifully with the trader's sinew line and bone hook baited with the guts of the previous fish caught. Snapper and drum and sea bass—they never got tired of the food and even adjusted to the unpleasantness of scaling and dressing the fish with the sharp, flaked flints in the trader's kit. Grilling took place on a stone slab set on a hearth built on a thick log section. Yanni wanted to catch the small sharks that swam up, but Terri restrained him.

Tracco traded in a class of high-value items that attracted their attention. He had a quantity of slender, abstracted human being statuettes with extended, distorted stone heads. Each statuette was about eighteen inches long, polished to a high sheen and made either of bright bluish-gray serpentine or olive-green jade. Terri knew the slaves and killers behind them produced the statuettes because she had seen some of them in the great courtyard in the circular family monuments. Terri marveled at the contradiction of a high artistic aesthetic stemming from a culture marked by immense brutality.

25

"I found more sage!" shouted Ah-noot. Kheeg-ah-tah went to her with his sharp flint and cut through a few bunches of the herb. They cooed and clucked as they examined the quality of the crop, collecting armloads of medicinals and other trance herbs while Faringway and Roller conferred.

"*Tck...tck.* We know trance is flexible and capable of superhuman power, but what is it?" Roller asked.

"Good one," replied Faringway. "You're so good at identifying problems. Now how about some solutions?"

"Thanks for your support, Faringway."

"I'm a little off balance by this situation, too, you know. I'm thinking that maybe impressions are as good as answers right now—just to let you off the hook."

Roller nodded telepathically.

Faringway laughed, "And my persistent mental image of that storm that blew us into the next universe had some features like this trance zone—the objects blowing out of that hurricane looked to be from different times, like what we see at different times in trance. And what are those giant hexagon shapes? There's an awful lot to sort out here."

Faringway raised his finger sharply to stop Roller from interrupting him, "No, Roller, look, Kheeg-ah-tah and Ah-noot are not from the same time period or even the same continent. Yet they found each other as trance allies easily through working with us. Either they have the immense power to move backward and forward in time—that immutable river—or else time is simply not what Western Civilization thinks it is."

It was Roller's turn to raise a punctuating finger. "Historical shamans told anthropologists openly that they could fly backward and forward in time. Of course, no scientific anthropologist would say they believed that or would investigate it further."

"Typical," Faringway said. "And one last thing, we think of the seers—Nostradamus chiefly—but the Oracle of Delphi and the Old Testament prophets as well, as predicting the future, but the remote viewers of the Eighties described the visionary process as *going* there and *seeing* it. And that's what Kheeg-ah-tah and Ah-noot have taught us to do."

"You're describing strong psychokinesis as part of the mix of abilities in trance traveling. Our shamans collect their herbs from the earthly realm, take them into the trance world, and return the material to their earthly camps for use there."

Faringway clicked his fingers twice. "Faster on the uptake, bub. In my few conversations with Ah-noot, she has already pointed out that the trance world intersects with material reality, what she calls the middle level, and there is probably an intersection at every point in those spheres. Tell that to your quantum physics friends, and don't ask me about the geometry of it. I'm not Newton or Feynman.

"But to push the oxcart of science a few feet farther along the road of knowledge, all the so-called psychic abilities or powers may be contained in some small, mostly undiscovered circuit in the human brain. It's a node in the mind that may interface with whatever is trance, activate that intersection in every human brain, and the rest is the future of humanity."

Roller was thoughtful. Ah-noot glanced over at him. Finally, Roller said, "We certainly can't argue with the shamans who have been gaining all their beneficial results from trance for thousands of years."

Ah-noot interrupted them, "Not all the results are beneficial. There are enemies in the overworld." She went back to scanning for herbs.

The men let that sink in. "Shamans are human, after all," Roller said reflectively. He felt his old fears coming back. "We should examine our motives in that light for sure."

"We should first agree on our common values," Faringway said. "We've always known each other as snarky rebel scientists. Maybe we should agree on our common purpose. Hell, maybe first we should find a purpose we can agree on!"

Bringing up a topic that sounded like sharing was so unlike Faringway. Was a peace treaty being offered? Roller laughed. "Agreed. I've worried about the other members of the team. Maybe they're in dire straits, worse than ours. No way they landed in a nice chair by the fireplace at home. Alan Silvy's probably dead, but what about the others? Perhaps we could search through the trance world with Kheeg-ah-tah's and Ah-noot's help?"

"It's not an option, it's more like a necessity at this point," Faringway said. "We don't know what the aftershocks of the Marfa event were. Was Earth destroyed? Was it thrown into a nuclear winter scenario with sunlight blocked? What was that event, really? And above all, will you still have to pay back your grant if you return to the same timeline?"

Roller roared. "Yes, we need all the living members of our team to piece it together and give it a kind of stereoscopic view."

"Yeah, we need to sort all of that out before we can think about going back to our home, if we even have a home."

"Or answer this question. What's 'home?'" Roller asked, looking at Ah-noot collecting an armload of orange and yellow wildflowers.

"We could bring Faringway to the camp now," Ah-noot said from behind a huge load of plants, herbs, and flowers, "but I don't have an extra fur robe for him to use. I'll have to make a robe for him."

"What are the flowers for?" Roller asked.

"My spirit animal likes them a lot."

"*Ay yi yi,*" said Roller.

A groan came from Faringway, while a joyous smile shone from Kheeg-ah-tah.

26

Weeks later, Ah-noot and Kheeg-ah-tah were more cautious in trance now. Ah-noot wore small power bundles tied on her special overshirt with large sea eagle feathers tied onto the shoulder yoke. Kheeg-ah-tah periodically threw small bundles of an herb out into the trance space. They chanted continuously and taught several chants to each other.

Roller was very happy to have found a new team, albeit one on a life and death mission with a highly uncertain outcome. He was amused, however, that Faringway was based at the mud hut camp when not in trance space with the shamans and Roller. He was mild and accommodating, unlike their time before the Marfa event. Roller had feigned jealousy when Ah-noot presented Faringway with a mink cloak she had made. He strutted around the camp preening in a fashion unbecoming a computer programmer until Roller mocked him and pointed out a couple of marten pelts in the cloak. Faringway laughed, unfazed, and delighted in discovering several interior pockets in the garment. Roller thought that was really out of character.

"We can search widely for your companions based on their names," Ah-noot said, "but that is very difficult without material objects or images that vibrate with their innate energy, as you know. As there are many timelines, there are many search channels, and all of them take energy. Remember, we found Faringway relatively easily because he was already traveling the trance world with Kheeg-ah-tah."

"You cannot forget that the dangers are out there," said Kheeg-ah-tah. "We found each other quickly. The longer we search, the more likely we will encounter hostile forces. My banes are only partial protection."

They had names of the team members but no other resonant energies of them. The first several searches were kept short as simple searches, in the Marfa timeline, in case Laney Joe, Terri, and Yanni had not been blown far. Then they branched out, first to Kheeg-ah-tah's timeline, since he knew of the Marfa Lights, and then more widely. They searched together and ended each session fatigued. Kheeg-ah-tah returned to the village wickiup and the others to the mud hut camp. Ah-noot moved them about five months ahead in her timeline, close to the beginning of spring in order to avoid the rigors of winter. The shamans could not neglect their healing duties, so Ah-noot went back to the village in the wintertime to check in with her people.

The suggestion of threat weighed on Roller. In trance, he saw no one; everyone he looked in on did not see him looking back. But he suffered nausea and a foreboding feeling of being watched. The feeling attached quickly to his old fears like an emotional vampire. He asked the others, but nobody felt anything out of the ordinary nor a possession spirit or entity.

Ah-noot spoke to him as they were about to come out of trance at the mud hut camp. *An entity may have entered your mind surreptitiously. I have several preventative banes I keep on my person that work against them.*

157

I must keep my identity secure against intrusion, and I feel poorly that I was not thinking of you and Faringway. Each of you shall have a small pouch of defensive power before our next foray. Kheeg-ah-tah calls them medicine pouches. He will make and bring more wolf's bane to surround us as well. Your team is important to us as well as to you.

Then Ah-noot's face softened and she leaned into him. *Know, my gentle one, that I will never leave you alone. If ever we are separated, I shall find you. We shall not be lost from each other for long.* Then they left trance and crooned to each other in what was becoming their private language. Roller slept with a sense of peace he had rarely ever felt in his life.

Days later, in trance and transit again, the group soared widely in several time dimensions. Animal life moved ecstatically in every channel. The monuments of humanity rose and fell in bannered newness and tree-sprouting ruins. The soaring visitors saw them without being seen. Ocean swells, tsunamis, and beach surf eroded the land, covered it, and created it fresh again. Mountain fogs condensed to rivulets, streams, and mighty rivers in an endless planetary rhythm. Forests challenged the sky and over time surrendered their green to gusty waterless deserts under the shifting of climate change. Life thrived in every timeline.

Roller and his new team did not forget their mission. They surveilled thousands of faces on Earth. They acknowledged other shamans at their work in the trance world. The human presence was strong in both realms. At first, the visitors did not notice a trance mover apparently on a similar mission. As the presence moved closer, Roller was the first to feel the lively spirit. Surely, it was Laney Joe.

Greetings and surprise stopped them all. Ah-noot and Kheeg-ah-tah greeted him at once and asked why they had not been told Laney Joe was a shaman. Roller and Faringway shook their heads. *We didn't know,* they said in unison. The Horus falcon soared confidently above them. Roller mused that in ordinary life now he might not have recognized Laney Joe, such are the changes a person undergoes when they discover who they truly are. He was robed and cloaked well for Egypt. His long garb emphasized his height. His beard was well-trimmed, and he had been keeping his hair short with bronze Egyptian shears. Roller felt pride that he had seen power and skill early on in Laney Joe.

Kheeg-ah-tah was the first to notice his wolf bane activating. Out in the trance space, sickly pink and green concentric rings emanated from places where bane had been set. Staticky white noise picked up in volume.

Ah-noot said, *We have to leave trance at my camp with Laney Joe immediately.* In order to keep the focus on Siberia, Ah-noot and Roller each took one of Laney Joe's hands.

They emerged from trance at the camp, outside the hut, but as they did, another figure materialized with them.

"Horemheb!" Laney Joe shouted in warning, identifying the figure in full Egyptian regalia brandishing a small black object in one hand. The entity appeared without his spirit familiar. "The black thing is a kill weapon!"

Horemheb looked intently at Laney Joe, his eyes glittering with predatory intent. He turned his weapon toward the others. Laney Joe focused his anger on the enemy while Kheeg-ah-tah and Ah-noot chanted defensively in unison.

Roller was almost paralyzed with the fear with which he had grown up, but now he was angrier at the fear than he was at Horemheb. The monster was looking for someone among them, or they would all have been killed immediately. And now Roller understood Ah-noot's calm and peace living alone among brown bears. She had rejected fear. Horemheb was looking earnestly at Ah-noot now with a kind of recognition, as though she were the one he really wanted.

Taking Horemheb's slight distraction as the last opportunity he might ever have, Roller launched a head-spearing blow into Horemheb's midsection and drove him back before the heavyset alien could sweep him aside like an annoying mosquito and kill him. The others rushed forward and piled on like football tacklers.

Thunder boomed and a bolt fell like lightning on Horemheb's gun hand. The real weapon, the Horus falcon, had found his opportunity, and his talons showered sparks like a diamond saw cutting a steel rail. Sparks flew like darts into all, leaving burn marks and igniting clothing. Everyone fell back, stumbling through the objects in the tiny yard outside the mud hut. Steam and smoke roiled upward from the two combatants as blasts of force pushed the human participants to the ground where they cowered as if from the onslaught of a tornado, bereft of all thought. Roller felt himself falling into the chaos of death.

Then, Horemheb raised a scream on a truly magical scale. His face and body contorted, and all his teeth pointed. Echoes returned from the forests and mountains. With an enveloping burst of flame, he threw the Horus falcon from him in a pulsating ball of feathers, then vanished. They knew Horemheb could enter and leave the trance world instantly, and it gave him tactical superiority. They also knew he had left this incident wounded and so might not be back soon.

Everything in the courtyard in front of the hut was overturned, the front curved and the side of the hut was dented with large, branching cracks in the mud surface. The forest all around the camp was now silent except for the gurgle of the snow-fed stream.

The Horus falcon rose in slow, labored flight and flew to Laney Joe, bating on his arm. The spirit familiar gently pecked both his cheeks several times. Each touch drew blood that flowed with Laney Joe's tears down onto his chest.

Kheeg-ah-tah took the falcon back into the trance world to minister to the very powerful ally. He knew many ways to help the bird, and it was clear to all that the Horus falcon was gravely wounded. The men were still looking around fearfully, not knowing what to do. Ah-noot herded them into the hut. Before she herself entered, she carefully picked up the long falcon feathers that were lost in the fight. Roller knew at once their life-saving power was immense.

27

Everyone lay flat-out in the hut, exhausted and fearful. Roller still shivered a bit but took comfort in the relative security of the hut as he looked for light cracks in the fractures in the mud facing from the inside. The back of his neck hurt miserably from head spearing Horemheb, but he exulted in being alive. He reveled in how doing the right thing had the most surprising outcomes, like surviving. Ah-noot clucked and cooed over Laney Joe's face, leaving him with a green poultice on both cheeks. Between the poultice and his beard, Laney Joe could have scared off Horemheb with a look. The others dabbed poultice on skin that had been exposed to the Horus falcon's sparks. Ah-noot gave the handful of feathers to Laney Joe, saying in her language, *hold these until I need them,* forgetting that they weren't in trance. Laney Joe got the message, anyway. Ah-noot built up the fire with a few sticks and crawled into Roller's cloak with him. The warm, smoky interior of the mud hut reassured Roller, as did Ah-noot next to him.

She learned much from the encounter with Horemheb. He was more powerful than any of them, and quite possibly they would all be dead soon. But in a very peculiar way she felt drawn to the struggle, knowing that she stood for the world and everyone in it against the cold unknown. She relaxed, ready for the struggle.

They rested a few hours and after they woke, started chatting among themselves while casting fearful glances at the doorway. Ah-noot, who awoke extremely thoughtful, was quiet with her fingers steepled in front of her face. Roller knew something bigger than Horemheb's last attack was coming, no doubt a supreme effort.

Faringway posted himself near the doorway, occasionally glancing out into the cold darkness. Here, he knew, were people who seemed to care for him and defended him when he couldn't defend himself. He mused, with an ironic chuckle, that maybe, at last, he had found a family of odd characters who were more magic than real, and perhaps he had found them at the end of all their lives. Odd that he had gone looking for the paranormal out of his spiteful nature—a poor, negative motivation, he realized—but without much effort, the paranormal had found him instead. He thought of the plot twist ending of so many pulp horror stories: "Get out of there! The monster is inside your head!" Faringway knew of many monsters in his head, but the alienating, push-off, scream-back-at-them monster had no more work to do. Difficulties in life were simply the rocks in the shallows that made the stream gurgle. They were easily steered past, even if his little canoe later wrecked on Horemheb, who might be his nemesis, or perhaps his Grendel. Faringway knew he was no Beowulf, but he finally had a group with which to rise or fall in the struggle. He silently recited all the chants Kheeg-ah-tah had taught him, trying to concentrate their energy inside the hut.

Soon, Ah-noot got up and set a stone cooking tray on the fire. She then pulled four strips of hare meat out of a suspended food bag and placed the strips on the slab. She turned the strips a few times with a stick while the fragrance of the meat drove everyone mad with hunger. Then, she clapped her hands once and held her arms apart in invitation.

Later, Ah-noot addressed Laney Joe, communicating that he needed to take them into trance with his ritual method. Roller joined in, telling him that Ah-noot was out of fresh indigo mussels.

"What?" Laney Joe asked.

"It's a molecule," Roller said.

"A molecule?" Laney Joe replied.

"Sorry, I'll explain some other time," Roller said.

Laney Joe brought out his equipment, explaining that he was out of candles. Ah-noot left to prepare a small torch that could be placed upright in the hut. With the bowl and tripod, he also produced the golden pectoral, which of course he had to explain immediately. Ah-noot reached out and touched it carefully and directed Laney Joe exactly where to place it. She got up and found some of Kheeg-ah-tah's leftover wolf bane and placed small bits in the cardinal directions around the pectoral and one large clump directly on it. Then with the rest of the bane, she left and sprinkled it in a light circle around the perimeter of the hut. Roller thought that was superfluous, as Horemheb already knew where they were, but he said nothing.

Roller, the perennial loner, somehow now only needed to observe, not keep an iron grip on control. He occupied himself with the details of survival now, knowing it may have many complications before it was secured. His confidence in Ah-noot was supreme. But if their survival was not secured, so be it.

They all entered trance, and Ah-noot got down to business. "We have seen all we need to know of Horemheb and learned all about him. He will return, and here's why. He wants to capture me for his own unearthly purposes."

Roller and Faringway both twitched at the word "unearthly."

Ah-noot went on, "His powers are beyond any earthly shaman's. He can enter and leave trance at will, he has massive defenses, and his small black death ray is actually a mind weapon. He only has to point it and think the words 'you die.'"

Laney Joe joined in, "He can see us remote viewing him, as he did at the royal court at Amarna when he killed my teacher, Lor-naat. He also found the Hall of Records, founded by the Atlanteans, looking for something. The Horus falcon is the guardian of that place and the falcon killed his spirit familiar—more reasons for the evil one to hate me."

Ah-noot pointed at herself. "He was looking for me, I am sure, but that was no mean feat for the Horus falcon, and I salute both of you. Horemheb also has side projects, if you will, in his mischief. Destroying you is just one of them. My clairvoyance is not enough to spy out all of his activities. Sadly, in our world, sometimes shamans lose track of their mission to heal the Earth and its life. The fallen ones, as I call them, abuse the great powers they have been granted, and they do so to elevate themselves. When he finds them, Horemheb hastens their corruption and piles up more bodies. This much I know. The fallen ones serve his mysterious purpose."

"I am his ultimate target in this realm of space. I have been revealed, or exposed, to him by our confrontation. I have the greatest shamanic power of any in several timelines, and I have many allies. Kheeg-ah-tah will readily agree to that. Perhaps Horemheb is a kind of gardener, weeding out the tallest plants so many more will grow without the tall one shading them. That's the kindest thing I can say for him. But it is more likely he is an evil shamanic vampire from another world. Somehow, I knew this day was coming."

Roller felt something twisting deep inside him. Long ago, he would have called it fear, but now he felt it was a deep, anxious caring for those around him he had come to love.

"Now, light hearts, to our plan," Ah-noot continued. "Know that every shaman of every type can be defeated and outmaneuvered. That is our deepest secret. She pointed at Laney Joe. "First, know that the golden pectoral was Horemheb's homing device on you, even though you think he never saw it. It was only chance that you and I were at the same place when he attacked. May I take it to a very safe place?"

"Of course," Laney Joe said.

"Very good," Ah-noot said. "We need to complete the mission fast before Horemheb can prepare his own plan against us. We will have to do our work while fending him off. It is ever thus. When we find Terri and Yanni, they must be brought here quickly. You have seen some of my defenses, but I think your Horus falcon will not be well enough to fight again soon."

Ah-noot took a deep breath. "But first we must find them. Laney Joe, do you still have any objects belonging to the woman or the boy, at least the woman because if the boy was separated from her, he could not have survived."

Laney Joe looked pained. "Not even gum wrappers in my pockets from either one of them. The clothes I wore when we were separated in the storm are long gone. I am in Egyptian linens now, and they knew nothing of them."

Ah-noot came closer. "Did you know that woman? I mean, did you *know* her?"

Laney Joe, whose life and character were shaped by brutal experience, blushed through his beard and forehead nevertheless. Mustering all the aplomb he could manage, he asked, "Does anyone ever really know their lover?"

Everyone nodded their heads and muttered in agreement, waiting for Ah-noot to continue. "That's good enough, young sir," she said. "You shall be the lead set of eyes looking for them—"

"I remember one thing, Ah-noot," Laney Joe said. "The boy, Yanni, was wearing a T-shirt at the time of our separation with a garish monster face on it. Terri wore all black at the time."

"Yes," chimed in Roller and Faringway.

"Good. Anything distinctive helps," she said. "The last set of things are very important. If we find them not in trance, we have to heave them through the worlds here to the mud hut camp. It will take all our energy to bring them here. But, then we must immediately launch them and us into your home timeline using the Earth energy of the camp with its earth, air, fire, and water. Believe!"

Even then she wasn't finished. "I will target you into the timeline a few years ahead of the time you left without apparent aging. That's a small benefit. The greatest one is dodging Horemheb and his mind killer."

"But what if the Marfa event destroyed the Earth?" asked Roller, trying to stop that persistent, small ping in his head.

"Then you are dead, and the Earth is fulfilled. If it remains, your lifetime mission from then on is the healing of all," Ah-noot said simply. Roller staggered at the power of the statement.

They came out of trance in the darkness of night, but even so, Ah-noot took Laney Joe's golden pectoral, inspected it for fastenings, and strode confidently off to the village to trade for some longer sinew cords for it she said.

Roller and Faringway left the mud hut to collect fuel for the next day's campfire. The starlight shone brightly as they worked. No moon shone to assist them. Roller felt a sense of completion, rightness, and harmony. Whatever the next day brought, he was content. He had built and lived in his mud-hut home and seen his psychic transformation completed here. Few lived lives as full as his.

The sun came up, and they made ready. A campfire was going outside, and Roller, Faringway, Laney Joe, and Ah-noot were on their knees in a semicircle around the fire, facing it, the stream, the forest, and the sky beyond. They left, Laney Joe leading them into trance, first to find Kheeg-ah-tah, but not before smudging the entire camp with sage.

Kheeg-ah-tah soon joined them, having left the Horus falcon on a branch at his wickiup camp. Most of his tribe had stood in a circle around the bird, a species unknown in their country. He knew the bird was safe, apparently enjoying in stoicism and stillness the attention of the humans.

Kheeg-ah-tah had information. He had seen a woman and a boy on a trader's canoe on the ocean in a timeline a few hundred years before his own. The boy wore a garment with a fearsome deity on it.

Laney Joe led them to the timeline, knowing with growing certainty that he was finding them. Dim memories of Terri grew brighter and stronger as the team sped closer. The small things—her touch, her hair, their first meeting, lovemaking under the Marfa moon—all grew sharper as he flew.

At last they looked down and saw Terri and Yanni eating grilled fish on a trader's canoe floating on the ocean.

28

Terri and Yanni finished eating their fish while Tracco paddled, and both felt a strong urge to nap. They slid down next to their wooden gunwale and relaxed easily into deep slumber.

Terri dreamed a sunrise, then another and another. Strands of clouds wrapped the suns, then streamed off over the horizon. The ocean rose and rose, merging with the sky in one fluid world. Forty-foot-tall stone giants stalked through the gel-like medium, their wide-open mouths booming. Yanni rode through on a shark, one arm waving like a bronc rider. Polished stone statuettes swam through in a sleek school like fish, one pausing to raise a stone arm in greeting. A vast, spinning ball of light threw off trees, flowers, a deer, jaguars, a falcon, a bear, small creatures she could not recognize, and many fish. People moved around easily. She saw Cho-lub spinning like a pinwheel. Far off, she thought she saw Laney Joe, and then the team leaders, Roller and Faringway. With them, she saw the faces of an Asian woman and a Native American man.

Terri heard her own voice in the dream saying, "The morning light through the limbs gnarling nirvanic completes the oneness we wish to share. I marvel, eyes closed, and open my chest while the flowers loft futile and proud into the arc of day."

The trance team collected Terri and Yanni in a powerful act of psychokinesis, the prelude to what Ah-noot held in store for them all, and they stole away to the Siberian camp. Tracco the canoe trader saw the two crewmen vanish into thin air. After a few months, he doubted his memories that the two had ever been on his canoe.

They left trance at the camp and moved with machine-like precision, leaving Terri and Yanni in their dream states after helping them recline in the circle around the fire. Ah-noot was out of fur robes or blankets, but Laney Joe placed his around Terri, and Kheeg-ah-tah threw his deerskin around Yanni. The fire was at its height, and the team took power with every breath of the cold air. Ah-noot began chanting immediately and took her place across the fire from the semicircle of celebrants. They all needed maximum energy because they were going to perform a supreme act of psychokinesis in returning to their home timeline and time period under Ah-noot's guidance.

Kheeg-ah-tah joined with Ah-noot and gestured for the others to begin. It was quiet, like a meditation circle in any other timeline. The circle of friends took up the energy of the elements, feeling the power of the earth beneath them. Peace reigned among them, if only briefly. The trees across the creek waved in the light breeze, bidding the voyagers farewell. Roller felt buoyant, happy where he was. Human beings strive to lose happiness, not gain it, and never realize it until it is too late.

Horemheb began to appear in reality, two steps behind Ah-noot. This time, he knew exactly where he wanted to be and who he wanted to capture, then destroy all the others, of course.

"SWEET FLOWER, COME!" The call by Ah-noot was a telepathic blast in everyone's head, followed by a roar like an artillery explosion in the forest across the stream. The sound was like a bear attacking, which it was.

Horemheb lunged for Ah-noot, reaching for the small black object in his pocket. As she dodged him, a gigantic bear broke out of the forest. It was an Ursus *arctos beringianus*, Latin for giant ugly bear, named Sweet Flower—Ah-noot's spirit animal.

The bear would have stood eight feet high at the shoulder, but this creature was speeding at a fast blur. The bear leaped the stream without touching it, landed on the near bank, and scattered rocks.

Horemheb spun around with his mouth wide open in terror, clearly too shocked to form any thought resembling 'you die.' Ah-noot's bear knocker seemed to come out of nowhere, and she took a desperate swing at Horemheb. The stone head just grazed Horemheb's arm, and the small black object, his murder weapon, flipped out of his hand and fell to the ground. A thin, long flaked chert blade flew into his right arm, thrown by Kheeg-ah-tah.

Sweet Flower stretched his mighty maw wide enough to engulf Horemheb's head, but the shaman dissolved out of his Egyptian linens and disappeared. Although Sweet Flower's jaws snapped shut on thin air, one huge paw sliced through Horemheb's linen garments before they hit the ground. The circle of trance people recoiled at the sudden violence. Terri and Yanni began to wake up and groggily looked around at their new unfamiliar surroundings. The fire continued burning down. Only a few flames danced in the circle of white ash that was growing thicker. The breezes were light, uncaring of the scene of violence, and somehow soothing.

The bear skidded to a halt with his forelegs wrapped around Ah-noot. He gave her one massive purple tongue lick from her neck to the top of her head. Ah-noot giggled, reached into his neck fur, and examined Laney Joe's golden pectoral to make sure it was securely in place in the sinew necklace around Sweet Flower's huge neck. The bear placed his wet nose directly on her mouth to check what she had been eating lately. One claw scratched behind Ah-noot's shoulder, the slight furrow just filling with red. Sweet Flower ambled off in the direction of the beach. Sweet Flower had been Ah-noot's insurance policy against Horemheb's return, and she didn't know if it would work. The group did not chant to seek Horemheb's return, but Ah-noot knew that with his near-omniscience in the trance world, keeping him away or hiding from him would present impossible tasks.

Laney Joe recovered his presence of mind first. "Continue the ritual, everyone. Horemheb can come back just as fast as he left." He directed the chant with both hands. Faringway chanted forcefully and encouraged Roller to join in.

The chant continued, much adrenalized. Ah-noot ran to her original position across the fire from the chanters. The spot was important, because they had arranged the four elements in a line away from the semicircle of chanters—fire, water, earth, and air beyond. It was how she focused the titanic energies of the Earth. Ah-noot made emphatic arm gestures with her hands shaped like bear claws, in sympathetic magic calling down all the powers of her spirit animals. It was a summoning of powers directed toward sending them all into trance and psychokinetically into the timeline they all recognized as home. Ah-noot had never felt so powerful. They all had to be in trance before they could transport. The energy draw would be immense.

They felt the lift of trance. Laney Joe directed Terri and Yanni in joining them, now that they were semiconscious. Ah-noot accelerated the pace of the dance of her arms. Roller felt himself leaving the camp. Laney Joe spoke out from deeper in trance, *Move from that spot, Ah-noot!*

It was too late. Horemheb appeared in reality directly behind her, this time naked, but with no lines of blood running on his arm. He threw his arms around Ah-noot and began to disappear. He'd appeared before anyone could react without his lost murder weapon, and his target for capture, not for killing, was Ah-noot. They heard the roar of Sweet

Flower, but he was too far away this time. The last image Roller saw of Ah-noot was only her two arms and hands continuing to choreograph and direct the group into trance and the portal into that world above their own. It was her greatest and most healing dance of ecstatic trance, and she was being removed from it.

But it was done. Suddenly Roller couldn't see the point of returning to the timeline of his birth. This was where he belonged. From now on, he would be a man without a home, without a country, without a family. How many human beings had called a mud hut their home? Millions and millions. And there was his mud-hut home below him, drifting away. His love and that which gave meaning to his life disappeared with it. The hut dissolved in his vision, wavy like rain down a windowpane.

Roller's last thought was, *Could I please stop thinking?*

29

When two or more trance movers enter the trance world, the exhilaration is heightened in order of magnitude, not merely doubled. The clarity of the world, the brightness of the sky and its stars, the pathways into those stars, the mysteries of its clouds and fogs and caverns, are all raised to a level beyond any lotus eater's imagination. The psychokinetic power is supersonic. When the two trance movers are fighting mortally when they enter the overworld, the peace of the space is held in suspense, and the most innocent of creatures in the earthly level pause and take cover.

Horemheb held Ah-noot's arms tightly out in front of her as he launched them both into the overworld. She struggled mightily as they flew rapidly away, far and high. Her attacker kept her hands away from her body, held rigidly to keep her from summoning her circle of shamans to rescue her—especially Laney Joe's falcon. He did not know that they had all gone away and could not save her now.

Ah-noot struggled in panic at his painful grip. She could feel a pattern of scales beneath his skin, clearly one mark of a creature from another world. She tried to scream telepathically for Sweet Flower, but she knew they fought well outside the range of his powers. Screaming felt good, so she continued it. She concentrated her physical energy against Horemheb, but his arms possessed snake-like strength, like the coils of a python. She used his weight against him, managing only to tumble the two of them in their flight.

Earth, stars, clouds, suns, oceans, and wind all spun around them in spirals as the two beings twisted and turned in flight through the sky of the trance world. The combined universe and its elements flashed and flashed, a kaleidoscope of reality crushing itself into smaller and smaller bits of matter, color, and light. The two trance travelers locked together could only drive themselves faster. Ah-noot clung to Horemheb as much as she tried to push away from him.

Tears and saliva squeezed out of her face when she tried to open her eyes and mouth. It was as though they were both strapped onto a moon rocket at launch. Her hair whipped in every direction. Horemheb's mouth gaped above her, showing his shark-like teeth. He continually shifted his grip on her like a wrestler seeking to find a winning hold or a constrictor trying to slip a second coil around a victim's body.

Ah-noot knew he wasn't trying to eat her; he had another purpose. If he was trying to make an ally of her, his approach was poor.

"You must obey," he said. "If you don't, the consequences will be severe."

"For me or for you?" she screamed back at him, pulling an arm free and slamming it into his belly. He didn't flinch.

Horemheb brought them back to a point high above Ah-noot's home village. Ah-noot didn't need telepathy to discern Horemheb's intent. He loosened his grip with one arm, and Ah-noot did the same. He hurled a curse like a bomb down to Earth with one arm, and Ah-noot quickly drove a punch into the forearm, the same one that had been struck by Kheeg-ah-tah's throwing knife. This deflected the energy flying downward into the village. The small portion of evil intent that struck the villagers caused them all to clutch their stomachs and double over. Ah-noot heard their moaning and crying from her height. She saw them crawling for shelter into the collection of mud huts that formed the village. A full blast would have killed them all.

Infuriated, Ah-noot realized she'd have much medical work to perform when she returned—if she returned. She kicked and jabbed Horemheb furiously to little effect. Then she remembered that his interior anatomy might bear little resemblance to that of mammalian bipeds. He only looked like an Earth human.

At that moment, she recalled the strength of the lowly worm, not mammalian, not reptilian, not vertebrate at all, but soft and flexible. The worm slowly works through the smallest space and continues its life journey, and its journey fertilizes all the soils of the Earth. Ah-noot chanted that thought several times, emphasizing life and fertility. She oozed out of Horemheb's arms downward and rose upright behind him.

Horemheb spun around and charged. Ah-noot backed away at high speed, drawing him away from the village before he could do more harm. They flew away at eye-blurring speed, facing each other.

"Help me, Ah-noot, your world needs it," he shouted.

"You cannot attack me for help," she replied.

"You don't know how to pay attention, Low One," he sneered.

He succeeded in creating a grain of curiosity in Ah-noot. Help? What was his real purpose? But she was not sufficiently curious to work or slow down to find out. He was the most harmful entity she had encountered in the trance world, and she had little experience of beings with even half of his power. It seemed like the evil entities, who would be called demons in other realms, were single-minded beings that only wanted to gain an advantage and exploit the trance world to achieve it. They possessed no love at all.

If Horemheb was an alien, he might not have a lot of critical knowledge about Earth and its life, although he certainly knew enough to destroy a lot of it and had traveled extensively on the planet. He had been terrified at his first sight of Sweet Flower. That thought became persistent as they soared like rockets through the sky of the overworld.

Horemheb was catching up gradually and starting to strike overhand blows at Ah-noot. She uttered the chant of the turtle, another creature he might not know much about:

I carry my hut on my back,
My back, my back,
I carry my hut on my back;
The storm can blow,
Can blow, can blow,
There is nothing I lack,
I lack, I lack.

Ah-noot bowed her back and looked down as though bowing her head to Horemheb. He rushed up to her, striking a mighty overhand blow to crush her and seize her, but his arm struck an invisible barrier above her and slid off a dome of energy. He lost his balance and tumbled into the trance air at their high altitude. He pumped his arms and legs in the fall, grasping for purchase anywhere. He bellowed before righting himself.

Good, she thought. He was not all-confident and all-powerful, as he might have seemed to his victims. The dome energy of the turtle had taken Horemheb by surprise. She fled at full power and changed course several times to throw him off and not allow him to return to the village. Thunderheads built up all around, lightning arched from cloud mass to cloud mass. Turbulence sheared through them to tumble the combatants without warning as they raced.

The Fractured Universe

Ah-noot knew that nobody on Earth quite understood Horemheb's dangerous purpose on the planet. It was clear he came from off-planet, and whatever he intended entailed casually killing any number of human beings. Ah-noot, perhaps the only shaman on Earth who could meet Horemheb in his own element, was at a disadvantage. She knew she was a powerful healer, and sometimes healing required a strong dose of self-defense. She flew even more purposefully and began the chant of the bear, her personal totemic symbol and species of her spirit-familiar, Sweet Flower. Here was a pathway to power. The wind shrieked by.

Horemheb had recovered from his loss of balance and pursued Ah-noot unerringly with his species' natural radar, like earthly bats and moths. The decisive moment was now.

Ah-noot slowed her flight, and Horemheb came on, the scale patterns under his skin showing clearly in relief. With a great booming roar, Ah-noot turned and closed with Horemheb, making long, loping bear leaps. Her arms, hands, and fingers arched and curved in great bear gestures. Horemheb had only enough time to draw in his limbs protectively before the collision. Ah-noot hit him at what seemed like supersonic speed, and flattened out against him with the air knocked out of her lungs. Sparks, fire, and smoke boiled out around the locked fighters.

Ah-noot drove him backward over and over as she cut at him with claws and fangs. Her jaws closed on his neck; his subcutaneous scales were all that saved him from a bloody death. His thin, smoking blood had an acidic taste in her mouth and throat.

He convulsed in pain but managed to throw off her attack, streaming smoke from his wounds. He knew to a certainty that Ah-noot was the powerful entity Lun had warned him about. His mind murder weapon would never work on her. He bellowed; his anger and pain echoed in great booms off the mountains on the horizon.

Ah-noot watched him fly erratic patterns around her while his wound-healing systems worked on his smoking flesh, and she saw below them a tunnel mouth, or gateway, and what might be an ordered pathway to another desirable space. It loomed open and mysterious, but they both knew it was well locked. Before the tunnel mouth fell into blackness, they both could see the huge hexagon panels set together to form the walls of the tunnel. It was clearly empty with no traffic in or out. Why would it have defenses—controlled access, no entry? There was nothing like it on the ordinary material Earth. Naturally, the feature would not be visible outside the trance state. Still, the mouth was heavily guarded by energy fields. Both of them were at the edges of their knowledge while they flew and fought above the gaping mystery.

Ah-noot gagged directly over the tunnel mouth, spitting and foaming at the mouth like a dog that has bitten a foul-tasting toad from her bite at Horemheb's neck, which was far nastier. Horemheb was disgusted by her mammalian vomit and didn't try to close on her physically. She knew she couldn't escape by flight. She'd impressed him with her power, but her energy was depleting, and she must not let him know that.

Ah-noot felt the impact of a sand grain on one of her legs, blowing in that powerful storm, in emphasis of Horemheb's thoughts. The flow of particles from the tunnel could be felt high above it. She knew that the particles were not energized sand, or there would be buildup of the stuff around the tunnel mouth or in a dunelike plume extending downwind of it. No, they were a form of energy either generated by the tunnel or channeled by it from another source.

"You as a creature of this space must find the way into it for me," he said. "Then I will fulfill the promise of your planet, but only you can avoid the barrier energy flow that reaches us even here."

Ah-noot chose not to disabuse him of the notion. "I am sure you, with all your powers, can enter the well," She chanted internally the song of the Siberian tiger, while she moved lower above the mouth of the chamber in the Earth. Darkness in the tunnel closed in about fifty feet below the mouth. The source of the flow of the particles was not apparent. At her height, she felt a few pin-prick strikes of the barrier flow. She moved around, looking into the tunnel, craning her neck and pointing out landmarks to herself as though remembering a pathway she knew, totally faking it. *Listen tiger, listen tiger, as the caribou runs....*

She felt a rise of the powerful strength of the tiger within herself. She wondered if it were too much, if she would destroy Horemheb with the power of the tiger. But then she knew that she did not choose this battle; it was visited upon her by Horemheb. If he took this risk and suffered harm, so be it. His blood was on his own head. But she also knew that Horemheb and his interest in the tunnels might be the key to solving their mystery. The vicious winds tore at them. Her clothing whipped. His stance was impassive and poised.

With the ears of a tiger, Ah-noot heard Horemheb's muscles launch his surprise attack. She swung her right paw with giant claws full into Horemheb's face. His face burst into flame, releasing flesh, scales, and a monumental bellow of pain, but his momentum carried him into her. His arms wrapping around her like a snake's coils.

Ah-noot's tiger faded with much of her energy. She knew in an instant that she needed help. She could only chant and pray to her ancestors.

The antagonists floated, locked together in pain, above one of the entrances to alternate, or parallel, worlds. They had given supreme efforts in their struggle. It was a moment of quiet in the heat of battle.

Ah-noot again felt as though she were looking down a well, but this was a well of generations, of time. She looked down past her parents and grandparents, great-grandparents, on and on through time. She pleaded for strength, power, agency—anything that would sustain her in her struggle for humanity and the life of the world. She could conjure many powers, but now all her generations must come together in superior will and power to overcome and dominate. Yes, she knew that was what she must have to overcome Horemheb. He would destroy everything she knew. No fulfillment, just destruction. Deeper and deeper, into the deep recesses of time, her request for power went on and on at the speed of mind.

The trance world around them seemed brighter and clearer the more it became tinged with fear. The sunlit thunderclouds billowed, lighting up internally with lightning while thunder boomed. Between the clouds the sky shone an intense azure. Perhaps the trance world was not so unlike the ordinary world, after all. Even with Horemheb about to destroy it, it was creation formed in beauty and seasoned with risk. Every flowering meadow has its predatory snake.

Then it seemed that her mind's eye became clouded and her mind's imagery obscured. A mass of fur and blasts of icy wind seemed to engulf her, then more and more gusts came. A look down an imaginary well of time had given her great bulk.

"Show me the way into the well," Horemheb groaned. His entire visage was smoking. His arms rippled with returning energy and a remarkable amount of self-healing. He was such a powerful entity psychically and physically. Through evolution, his reptilian heritage gave him advanced powers of tissue regeneration. Ah-noot had seen frogs and salamanders that regenerated limbs.

Ah-noot knew that this was the moment that led to her life or to her death. She felt as though she was outside herself looking in, and her eyesight and mind's eye clouded. She held tightly to her consciousness and focused on her iron will. She knew she would likely die in any successful effort to destroy Horemheb. She felt that she stood in front of all her ancestors and all of humanity facing the beast that comes out of the dark. This one was a world destroyer from off the planet. He would not merely inhabit children's nightmares, he would actually destroy the world. Any entity who could master the trance world could easily control all the levels of Earth. She sorrowed for the children, for the whales, and for the bears. She knew this was simply the price expected of her for gaining the knowledge and power that had made her the premier shaman of Earth. She thought of every flowery herb she had applied to a sick child's face. She thought of Roller, how he was a flower that had only started blooming. Some burdens are lifted off one's shoulders and given to others to bear even when one's work remains unfinished. Clearly now was the time for her heavy burdens to be removed and for the Earth to go on in the hands of others. She felt their weight lightening with the thought. She stood ready with all her fear gone. "The pathway is straight down the center of the well," she said.

She felt shame that her last words had to be a lie. "You will be unharmed taking the leap."

She heard his cynical laugh. "Of course not, weak one, but you will take that leap, not me. All I have to do is test the barrier flow with a toss of a rock into it—you'll do nicely—observe it, and report back. Then your planet is ours forever, and I shall rule it."

Ah-noot summoned all her energy, preparing to lock with him and throw them both together into the abyss. He would not be expecting the maneuver, and it would be over before his powers could counter it.

He tossed his head back for another laugh, but his eyes bugged wide, and it seemed he screamed loud enough to be heard around the planet. Two giant tusks swept him to the side, off-balance, into the barrier flow, and a long snout issued a trumpet blast loud enough to pursue Horemheb's scream.

Ah-noot and her ancestors in the boreal plains of Siberia had conjured a wooly mammoth. The ancestors had heard and offered the concentrated power of all their generations of being. The support was spiritual and overwhelming. Horemheb fell wounded straight into the well mouth, his arms and legs pumping, unable to recover. He was in the particle blast with particles roiling around him and continuous sparking all over his body as he fell.

She heard a hearty laugh from directly above her. Oddly, Horemheb's body, spread-eagle in the barrier, slowed and stopped at a level of continuous glowing flames. Then his body rose to a level of dancing sparks that Ah-noot could see firing and playing all over Horemheb's body.

The mammoth faded, and Ah-noot floated, clearing her head and vision and staying firmly in trance, floating in the overworld, glorying in life.

She heard another laugh above her, this time a melodious giggle. She became aware of another entity, one of great power and brightly lit all around.

"I am Lun of Thonlus," the entity stated out of a bright coronal aura, "and I am the birth mother of Horemheb. Your world is very attractive to many, and the Meno, our people, have been honored to explore it for purposes of governance and mining, but—" she sighed and went on, "Ah-noot, I respect and honor you. Your defeat of my son has shown me more than I expected to see of your powers."

Lun was arrayed in streaming imperial brocades, billowing out from her like flags. She moved from directly above Ah-noot to a more conversational angle. Ah-noot could just see part of a bayonet scabbard strapped to one of Lun's calves above a delicate ankle. Lun looked at Horemheb and his body rose higher in the column of particles, to the level merely of extreme pain. Lun chatted while he writhed.

She sighed. "Sometimes manipulating a child in this way is the only way to retrieve the good from him." She smiled at Ah-noot. "We shall both benefit from what has happened here."

"There is a reason the many universes are discrete," she went on. "There are vast energy rivers flowing between them that serve as barriers. The secret to them is unknown to us. The Aat don't even know, and that's why they are so interested in your solar system. The Aat are godlike beings farther above us than we are above your species. We are barely advanced enough to gain their cooperation. They reach down and give us small projects of interest to them just to encourage us. Maybe they are supremely bored artists merely looking at us as one entertaining game."

"Really," sniffed Ah-noot. "That sounds purely decadent to me. Ask them to pull their own chestnuts out of the fire on their next 'small project,' and see how they respond."

Lun laughed explosively for several seconds. "The gamble might pay off like roulette. The Aat might destroy us at any time simply in the joy of finding a new prime number. What might they do with your sassy comment? Ha! They might make you the empress of a star cluster! Ha-ha!"

"Don't let them know I'm here," Ah-noot replied.

"Very well. Just be aware that the Aat and the Meno of Thonlus are fascinated with your planet. We are astounded at the beauty and patterns of your world. There are mysteries and variations, too. The energy fountain that so fascinated your lover seems to have been a device of some misbehavior by the Atlanteans. They, by the way, are pretty mysterious themselves. They seem to have been humanoid, but we are not quite sure where they came from—or where they went."

Lun's blue auroral plumes, matched by the brocade, shown like solar flares. "What is clear is that at an important level, Horemheb's mission has ended in failure. The Aat will not be displeased—the Meno having served due diligence and all that—but the Rrrl' will add the Aat's performance in this star sector to their list of grievances.

Ah-noot, for you, this means the Earth will be free from outside interference for thousands of years. You could be its queen," she laughed. "But that is clearly not the kind of power you seek or need."

Lun looked about her, smiling, "Such a lovely planet! I shall remove H-boy now. He won't disturb your world again. Keep seeking that thing you call love."

She moved away, and Horemheb rose from the barrier stream. Together, they flew rapidly up and away in an arc, Lun glowing in streaming light, a sparkle falling from her and Horemheb trailing in smoke.

Ah-noot remained silent for a few moments, trying to take it in and fight off exhaustion. She knew deep inside that she had passed her supreme test. She needed to lie fallow, like a lavender patch picked over too much. Then, of course, she must stand ready for the next challenge. She thought of Roller, knowing he would be proud of her. She rushed off to gather some herbs she knew she would need and tore off to her village to heal all the villagers.

30

Ah-noot had put them down in their own timeline in the middle of
urban North America. When they first tried to draw money from
their old accounts, they learned that they had been declared legally dead
after the Marfa event. Fortunately, they were able to easily prove their
identities and access their resources. Faringway had been greatly entertained at the time. "Now Berkish can't find us, and they can't get their
money," he said with a spiteful laugh.

Now he and Roller sat at the manager's table in Faringway's newish
restaurant, Late Archaic, on a side street with lines of patrons around the
block. They couldn't get enough of Kheeg-ah-tah's mudbucket cactus wine.

The region around Marfa and most of Presidio County, in which
Marfa had been set, had become a blackened lava field as a result of the
event. Anyone lost in it at the time would never have been found, unless
they had been blown into different timelines, and then only if they
wanted to be found. The event had set off a minor nuclear winter, with

a lowering of worldwide temperatures about two degrees for two years. World agriculture was just now coming back into high productivity. An active volcano in the Chisos Mountains of Big Bend still spewed ash and smoke.

"I see you've adapted well to harsh experience," said Roller, drawing from his straw in the center of the mudbucket.

"I suppose so," the exhausted Faringway said. "Really, the tough part since coming back was scaling all of Kheeg's recipes up to restaurant grade. But things are beginning to taper off. Kheeg spends most of his time on the streets expounding on peace and harmony in his strangely accented English."

"This year's flavor of the week is next year's distant memory—and we need more peace and harmony," Roller agreed. He glanced from side to side, cueing Faringway to do the same. "The city police have signed the new contract with us. They like our work."

"Great," said Faringway, "don't forget Laney Joe's talk tomorrow."

"Right," Roller said. "I'll have the turtle."

The next day, the door of the hotel conference room was open as Roller approached it. Loud voices in debate spilled out into the carpeted hallway. The announcement card on the easel beside the door read:

Friends of the New Kingdom

presents

Was Akhenaton Assassinated?

by

Lanford Joseph Y.F. Ferguson

Egyptologist, falconer

The world certainly hadn't ended for Laney Joe. He had returned to the familiar with a sense of purpose and commitment none of the others had showed. Knowing the dynamic, technical world insisted on credentials and licensing, Laney Joe enrolled in community college classes, mostly as cover for hanging out his shingle as an Egyptologist and offering lectures for pay. His real mission, of course, was to find Horemheb. He could only dream that Horemheb would walk into one of his lectures with his falcon, Horace, sitting on his perch attracting ticket buyers. Laney Joe's forays into the trance world were now confined to this timeline and planet Earth, and they were somewhat defensive, looking for enemies as much as for allies. They also frequently supported Faringway's and the team's enterprises.

Roller walked into the conference room and saw Terri and Yanni sitting near the back in matching camouflage garb. Terri waved him over, and he sat down. She held a finger to her lips for quiet. Yanni punched him in the belly and he responded by giving Yanni a Dutch rub. Yanni faked an open-mouthed scream.

At the podium in the front of the long, narrow room, Laney Joe was making quips while fending off angry verbal attacks. Horace ignored it all from his perch a few feet to the side of the podium.

"General Horemheb was the savior of the Eighteenth Dynasty!" the speaker, a professor at a small elite college, said. He was a "real" Egyptologist. He wore a twenty-years-out-of-date suit with a beard and spectacles to match. "The hieroglyphs all say that."

"Yes, the glyphs that weren't chipped out of the monuments along with Nefertiti's cartouches said that," Laney Joe answered. He was dressed in jeans and a shirt with many pockets. "Do you think some dissenting opinions might have fallen into the sand beside her name?"

"Horemheb was simply not a cold-blooded killer and evil magician," the professor declared.

Faringway, sitting near the front, turned and gave the man The Glare. "Had you asked any surviving Syrian, Hittite, or Nubian at the time, you would have learned that General Horemheb killed plenty," he said. "And the monuments do show that he had lust for power."

"If he wanted power, why not take it from Akhenaton's body after his evil deed and just step up onto the throne?" asked the professor.

"The royal court at Amarna had many friends after Akhenaton's demise," Laney Joe said. "At least that's what I saw…learned…in my research. Akhenaton had a co-regent, Smenk-ka-re, as well, who became pharaoh after Akhenaton, but he only lasted a year on the throne. No word as to why so short a time. Then the famous teenager Tutankhamon ascended the throne but died before he reached twenty-one years of age. Then the very poorly known Eye, or Ay, had a year of power and glory as pharaoh. Then General Horemheb ascended the throne and reigned for thirty years. I ask you: was Horemheb waiting his turn, or did he hurry things along?"

The room erupted in shouting.

Laney Joe laughed and waved at Faringway and Roller and winked at Terri. Then he waved for quiet and eventually got it. "I admit there is much we still don't know about Horemheb, but my research is directed toward finding out. A small mystery: Horemheb's tomb was found in the delta and fully excavated in the early twentieth century. Like many tombs in Egypt, no sepulcher was found in it. But the way the stones were cut, carved and assembled—I know something about that—the space was never designed or built to hold a sepulcher or coffin. It is a fake tomb, but with walls covered with hieroglyphics glorifying Horemheb."

"Off-world warlock!" shouted Faringway. The room erupted again.

Faringway and Roller had switched the research focus of the old team from ghost hunting to remote viewing in the tradition of Nostradamus. Terri joined Faringway's new team after she was trained in trance by Laney Joe, but she cautioned Faringway on a couple of points: they had to keep their investigations in this timeline and on this planet.

The police work of finding lost children and solving crimes, just now being organized, seemed like a great career path for Terri. Contentment fell on her like a blanket after she and Laney Joe married. Plain vanilla life was fine with her. She didn't need any more wild adventuring, but she remained ready for anything.

Terri leaned toward Roller and spoke in a low voice under the general hubbub. "Did you sign the mega-tablet contract, Roller?"

"Yes," he said, "and I kept the four patents I hold on it. The company is a small start-up just dying for an advanced product to market. They were willing to give me a good deal on producing the mega-tablet, with upgrades, from the blueprints." He still didn't know what had happened to the original mega-tablet. He assumed it had been destroyed at Marfa.

Roller's good news didn't really make him happy. He had lost his treasure and his love, and he remained a man without a planet. More painfully still, he had that feeling of not knowing which way to turn, exactly the same as when he woke up on that Siberian beach before he met Ah-noot. He dreamed every night of Ah-noot's fractured mud hut, melted to nothingness in ravening time, no doubt, but when it stood it had been his portal to the farthest stars. He could not visit the site, considering that Horemheb knew it, and he only wished that Kheeg-ah-tah could find or invent some effective Horemheb bane. Not having heard from Ah-noot after her confrontation with the monster, Roller feared the worst.

"Something else," Terri said, leaning toward him. "Look at this." She handed him a large brochure.

"Paris Fashion Week?" Roller asked.

"Read here," Terri directed him to the schedule of events.

He read, "With the banning of bear hunting in Russia, fashion designers present Siberian Chill: Nouveau Fashions in Fur. I'll bet they do this every year," he said.

"Read the list of designers, dumb-ass," said Terri.

Roller saw it instantly: Rolla Ahnutekova. She was broadcasting her location.

Terri dropped tickets on Roller's thigh. "My compliments. Same-day tickets for the hypersonic to Paris. They fly six times a day; you've already missed two flights."

Roller was glad he was sitting. "Are you and Yanni coming?"

"No. The SUV is loaded. We're picking up LJ and Horace after this. Faringway may come, too. West Texas awaits."

Roller scooped up the tickets and brochure. He stood up and walked out of the room, his heart leaping.

31

"Leo, Leo!" cried Salai, a boy running toward the stream. The day was sunny, and the boy looked for his patron where he had wandered beside the water. Salai saw the man sitting in his cloak beside a cascade on a small brook.

"Leo!" he cried again as he ran down to him. "Leo, you always ignore me and don't care about me at all."

Only then did Leonardo look up from the wavelet patterns in the pool he was observing. He had been holding a long, crooked stick in the water. His eyes came back into focus when he turned to the boy. "Salai—what did you steal this time? Why do you continually interrupt my work?" The man sighed and shook out the last of his mental cobwebs. The behavior of water was one of his continuing interests, and not just when storms around Milan freshened the streams and river.

Salai snorted. "Work! You are a daydreamer just like me. If you could actually finish more of your paintings, we'd be rich. Anyway, I didn't steal this time. I found this strange thing next to a dead man with one leg off up the hill. The man is dressed oddly, too." Salai was famous for pulling tricks on everyone around him, especially Leonardo, who had pulled him out of the magistrate's grip more than once. Most of the charges had been for stealing fruit from the sellers in the piazza, but once it was for selling some of Leonardo's ornate clothing after Leonardo found his wardrobe half empty. Leonardo was careful not to allow any of the street boys Salai always befriended inside their household. Leonardo, an indulgent creature, was gradually housebreaking Salai.

"French spies are everywhere these days," Leo said. "If the constabulary finds them, they cut off their heads, not their legs. Let's look at your 'strange thing' first."

Salai handed Roller's mega-tablet, stolen by Alan Silvy, to Leonardo da Vinci. The object was unlike anything seen by any Italian at that time period. It was a box of high-impact plastic, which Leonardo took to be some form of metal. There were hand straps, easy to figure out, and a kind of folding fabric covered a glass window. And wonder of wonders, through the window they could see images that moved. But the movements of things weren't in the northern Italian meadow behind the window as Leonardo held it. The view was of a strange, arid landscape at night. Dim lights appeared, moved, and faded. Occasionally, the scene shifted to a different night, but with the same mountains in the distance.

Leonardo was entranced immediately, but wisely decided not to operate any of the buttons on the device. Some of the lettering on the buttons looked like English, but Leo wanted help in learning the play of the device. He uttered one name out loud, "Bramante. We should take this home right now and not tell the constabulary about it," he said.

They walked across the meadow to Alan Silvy's body, his missing leg was about ten feet away. They couldn't tell much from his clothing—cotton trousers, leather shoes of unfamiliar make, and a shirt of very tightly knitted fabric. The man and the boy did not touch the body. It looked as though the amputation had just occurred, and the body was dropped there from an unknown height. A small amount of blood had oozed out of the stump and leg and started to congeal in the grass. Leo and Salai walked around the body looking for footprints, wheel tracks, other blood splashes, or any other signs of violence. The soil was moist from rain and would take prints easily.

"Nothing around it but our footprints," said Salai.

Leonardo jerked upright with a fearful look on his face. "We have erred!" he cried. "We must leave immediately! If we tell the constables and game wardens about him, they will accuse us of killing him and take us before a magistrate. There is no evidence except our footprints just now, so innocently printed. Hurry!"

That night, Leonardo and friends sat at the large corner table of their favorite tavern. The establishment stood down the street from the Old Ducal palace, where Duke Ludovico of Milan housed his subjects of patronage. Everyone at the table had quarters there.

In the tavern, Leo sat at the round table with his back to the room, wearing his cloak spread widely so the table couldn't be seen easily from elsewhere in the room. Donato Bramante held the mega-tablet, his eyes and fingers flashing all over the object.

"There is machinery inside the box that brings forth the pictures," Donato said. "How the pictures are made to move I don't know."

A cheer rose from the table. Leo voiced the sense of it, "This is the first time ever Donato Bramante, the designer of basilicas, has ever said 'I don't know.'"

The talk rolled far into the night, and the wine flowed. Leonardo was exceedingly thoughtful the whole time. "Perhaps time and space are not what we think they are," he said.

Hours later, Leonardo's chamber overlooking the courtyard in the palace was still lit by a single candle. Salai looked in on Leonardo, asleep on his bed with the candle shining on a writing desk, as usual. A large frame mirror was set up behind the desk, facing it.

Leonardo's current notebook lay open in front of the mirror. Leo had been working in mirror writing, as was his habit, the words were clear and cogent viewed in the mirror but backwards on the page. Moonlight from the courtyard competed with the candle to provide illumination.

Salai approached the desk to extinguish the candle. The odd device was locked away securely and nowhere in sight. In the notebook, Leo had drawn a picture of a long stick in a pool of water. The ripples flowed outward, outward, outward....

The End

Acknowledgements

Few works in any branch of art rightfully claim birth from only one creative human spirit. And *The Fractured Universe* is no exception. From the time I first explained my absences from my circle of friends by saying I had started writing a novel, I received great, unstinting encouragement from that circle. Foremost was Aralyn Hughes, who taught me all the ways to reserve my writing time, become more disciplined, and above all, "get your butt in the chair." Hughes sent me to Steve Adams, a world-class writing coach and Michener Fellow with the 2015 Pushcart Prize and many publications to show for his efforts and mark his talents. My gratitude to these two human beings knows no bounds.

Ditto Aralyn Hughes' Austin Tuesday Morning Coffee group, all of whose members humbled me with their praise and support. Valarie Varee Alexander and Mary Kay Klev took the time to write reviews and notes on early drafts and implore me to improve, please, improve my writing. Norma Jost, CK Carman (celebrity DJ of KUT-FM's "Cross Currents" jazz show), Christine Gilbert, and Sue Bires gave verbal encouragement on a near-constant basis. Sandy K. Boone, screenwriter and director of *J.R. "Bob" Dobbs and the Church of the SubGenius*, gave incisive industry insider advice and shared it freely. To all in the coffee group—thanks for the advice, collegiality, support, and friendship. If I misspelled anyone's name, I'll correct it in the next book.

Farther out from this circle of friends, Michael Meigs, webmaster of ctxlive.com, Carol Lewis, and Bettie Barton Buchanan of the Sayersville Historical Association, wrote reviews and comments on the final draft. Their thoughts on *The Fractured Universe* are available on Amazon. Their many creative kindnesses to me are very much appreciated.

Nicole Jeffords, novelist, portraitist, actor, and website manager gave inspiring encouragement in just a few words. They came at just the right time.

The giants of my education, whose knowledge and wisdom are reflected variously in *The Fractured Universe*, are Richard P. Schaedel, James A. Neely, Denise Schmandt-Besserat, and Richard N. Adams. They continue to lead me onward and upward.

Lightning Source UK Ltd.
Milton Keynes UK
UKHW012341140322
400044UK00003B/1007